TOUCHED BY DADDY'S 4 DIRTY FRIENDS

AN AGE GAP CONTEMPORARY REVERSE HAREM ROMANCE

THEIR TEMPTATION
BOOK SIX

BARBI COX

Copyright © 2022 by Barbi Cox

All rights reserved.

No part of this book may be reproduced in any form or by any electronic or mechanical means, including information storage and retrieval systems, without written permission from the author, except for the use of brief quotations in a book review.

This book is a work of fiction. Any resemblance to persons, living or dead is purely coincidental.

SOPHIE

I stare at the stack of wedding magazines my mother got me. As if things aren't all online anymore. I rub my temples and can feel the rings on my fingers brush each other. Glancing at my very heavy left hand, I feel heart-soaring love but also pressure.

We're down to six weeks now. I got the guys their rings, simple bands, but I tried to take time to pick out a specific one for each of them. It's been the least stressful thing on the To-Do list Mom made for me. Dress shopping, choosing a color scheme, writing four sets of vows, choosing an officiant, sending out RSVPs, and getting décor set up for the venue. Oh, and finding a place for the reception. So much to do.

And nowhere near enough time to do all of this work and stay sane. Let alone have sex or go on dates with my men. I groan and let my forehead drop to the table. Maybe the pain will do me good. But my forehead hits something soft and warm.

"Lucky you, I'm here to help with the venue décor," Gunner murmurs. "Can't do that if you're knocked out, Sweets."

"I don't want to do this. Can we go take a bath?"

"If we can bring the magazines," he murmurs.

I groan and let him pull his hand back. He kisses the top of my head and rubs down my neck, over my shoulders. I melt into his touch, wanting to lose myself in his hands, his touch, him.

"Let's procrastinate and do something fun."

"Like you?" He chuckles, kissing my earlobe, then nibbling. "If we make a few choices, I'll reward you with an orgasm."

"You're going to bribe me into planning our wedding?" I lean back to look at him.

He brushes my hair from my face and kisses my forehead while rubbing my jaw. "I like to think of it as mutual pleasure. Just … delayed."

"Are we sure we want to do this in six weeks?"

"Honestly, I'd be happy with us just having a reception and doing everything else in private, but now your mother is involved. Make her do all this," he whispers. "I'll be the devil on your shoulder. Just fuck us nonstop, show up for the dress thing, say yes to whatever, and drown yourself in ecstasy."

I hum in my throat. That sounds so much better than all this planning. But … but it's going to be my only wedding. I'm making sure of that. And it's important. I want the guys to know how much I love them, how much they are worth to me, all of that.

And as easy as the option is to let Mom handle it all, I feel like it would bother me in the long run or make our wedding less meaningful if we don't have our say in it. Gunner arches an eyebrow.

"So, what's it going to be, Sophie? You want to go have fun in bed or mark some shit before sending it to your mom so we can compromise?"

"I guess we should go through some of these." I motion to the magazines. "And decide what kind of reception we want: indoor or outdoor."

Gunner and I go through the magazines. I found a mini sticky-note pack that has five colors, so that way all five of us can leave input on things we like–other than the dress. That is for me and me alone. They aren't allowed to have even a hint.

Gunner looks at décor options for both indoor and outdoor and I look at venues that are close to the Monet gardens. Then I come to a complete stop. Gunner rubs my thigh. "What, Soph?"

"How are people going to afford to travel and everything to be at the wedding? Hotels, flights, paying for food." I shake my head and run my fingers through my hair.

"We will not leave them high and dry, Sophie. We'll book the rooms for those who RSVP and pay for them. Your bridal party will have their flights paid for and it's not like we'll need gifts. We can do a dinner event the night before instead of a rehearsal dinner, and pay for breakfast before the wedding, and breakfast the day after."

"But-"

Gunner pulls me onto his lap. "We are all richer than we can ever need to be and I see nothing better to spend money on than our wedding day."

"The honeymoon," I grumble.

He chuckles and kisses me. The heat from his mouth spreads across my body, even down to my toes as they curl. I'm left panting when he draws back. Gunner cups my face in his hands.

"Oh, you don't need to worry about that. We'll just get some awesome Airbnb and stay in bed all day until you decide you want a break from us." His low velvety voice makes my stomach fill with excitement, lust, and need.

How long has it been since I've been with any of them, let alone all of them? The night they proposed? No, after that. It was before we all met up with my dad to tell him. Gunner taps my nose. "I see that threat of Naughty Sophie. Put her away until we can put her to use."

I pout. "You said after we made some choices."

"Have you made any choices?"

"No." I glare at the computer. "I'm trying to figure out a hotel. I think that's the best place to have a reception."

He helps me look at hotels and we book mark three of them. One has the option for indoor/outdoor depending on the weather and then an outdoor and an indoor. I don't care as long as we're all happy. That's what's important to me.

Gunner shows me the décor options he likes and we talk about a few others across the magazines. I don't know if it's the illusion of productivity or the real thing. I just know we're getting somewhere.

We get more than enough done to earn me a solid make-out session. I moan into his mouth as our tongues tease each other. Gunner palms my ass and then pushes my skirt up to my thighs until he can tease me with his hand between my legs.

Two fingers press right against my clit and he rubs forward and back as my hips grind down on him. I moan and hide my face against his shoulder. "That feels good," I whisper.

"This doesn't look like wedding planning," Nick says, making me jump.

Gunner just pushes my damp panties to the side and keeps playing with me, circling my clit with two fingers until I forget whatever I was about to say. Nick picks up a magazine and huffs.

"What if–to keep things simple–we select an arrangement of flowers from the garden? Then the color can just follow that. Plus, it will give each of us grooms a different colored tie to wear so we can match—somewhat while still looking upscale."

"Sounds good." I gasp as Gunner sinks two fingers deep inside me and kisses across my neck. "So good."

"I think you're good at making decisions like this, Sweets," Gunner purrs in my ear before biting my throat. "What else, Nick?"

"Hotel two is the best option. Indoor and outdoor, just in case. I'm sure Roman will agree. He's all about being practical," Nick says. "Now, for the cake, we could have four flavors, just for fun. Four tiers."

"Fuck!" I whimper. Gunner knows just how to move his fingers inside me, hitting that pleasure button over and over like it will earn him a treat. I pull at his shirt, sending buttons scattering so I can kiss his chest. In return, he rubs my clit with his thumb. "Yes."

"We can add that to the list, then. I have a friend who has a bakery. I'll call him and set up a time for us to meet," Gunner agrees.

I don't know if it's the fact that things are getting done, or that Gunner is so unashamed of what we're doing, but this may be the best he's ever made me feel with his fingers. He drops me onto the table, drags my underwear down, and pushes a third finger inside me while spreading my legs.

"What do you think about lighting, Nick? Fairy lights like when we proposed candles? Maybe those color-changing lights?" Gunner asks.

Nick pulls off my shirt, then kisses me, his tongue lazy and slow despite how hard I pull him down on me. "What do you think, Sophie?"

"No candles," I gasp. "Yes, to the other two."

My back arches as Gunner ups the pace. He bites the inside of my thigh. "So many decisions, Sophie. I told you—all you needed was the right inspiration."

The second that Nick pinches my nipple, I come apart, yelling myself hoarse. Another hand strokes my hair and I see Holden. He looks me over. "I like this style of wedding planning."

"You should weigh in with an opinion," I hum.

Gunner rubs his wet fingers across my bottom lip, then pushes them deeper, across my tongue, so I can taste myself. Holden looks at the list of things we still have to decide. "We need to get these invitations out. We should make lists independently, then cross out the overlaps so they only get one invitation. Then we can book at the hotel."

Nick takes Gunner's spot, but sits down and drags my knees over his shoulder. He kisses along the inside of my thighs. "We'll need to make sure that we can get that as our venue before we book rooms there."

"I can call in a few hours when they open," Holden murmurs, then makes a note to himself.

Gunner pulls his fingers back and undoes his slacks. "I don't think you need your mouth right now."

I shake my head.

Gunner strokes over his hard cock before offering it to me. I take him eagerly, wrapping my lips around the head, then teasing him with my tongue. When Nick kisses my mound, I whimper and take more of Gunner down my throat.

Holden holds the back of my head in one hand and teases my nipple with the other. He sets the pace for me while also driving me insane. Nick eats my pussy, using his tongue and mouth in a wicked combination that has me moaning around Gunner's length.

I don't think any of us are focusing on wedding planning and I can't say I care. We've made more decisions in these last fifteen minutes than I have in three weeks. I make Gunner come right before I finish again, then Nick flips me over. He thrusts into my pussy while I take Holden deep in my throat.

My eyes roll back as I bounce between them. Gunner tells me what a good girl I am, and mumbles something about how unimportant the forks and plates are. He makes a few notes and by the time Nick, Holden, and I all finish, I feel recharged and ready for making some serious decisions.

Holden reminds me not to worry about the price, for the tenth time, then kisses my forehead and grabs his own magazine. Nick keeps me on his lap, still buried inside me, and grabs a magazine.

They talk to each other as I go get a shower and consider what our wedding is going to look like. Even in my fantasies, I see nothing but a fantasy because that's what I'm getting by marrying these four men.

Hmm, maybe some little white trees could be in the reception hall. To sell the fairy-tale theme.

"Look at me. Making choices." I tell my reflection as I pull on a dress. "Like a real bride."

NICK

Holden books the reception hall and Sophie makes a list of people. Gunner keeps flagging things in décor and that leaves me to think about the menu. Until Roman gets home. Every day, I swear he gets more exhausted.

Sophie lets her pen drop and goes to him, kissing him and purring Italian against his lips. He hugs her and kisses the top of her head. When he jumps and Sophie gives a naughty smile, I'm sure she's grabbed his ass.

"How was your day?"

"Long," he grumbles, then notices all of us at the table, going through magazines, except the ones that Sophie put to the side. "And it looks like it's getting longer."

"Don't you worry," she says. "I ordered dinner and you can rest for a while, okay?"

He rubs the back of his neck. "I don't want to be left out of the planning."

"And I don't want you overworking." She puts her hands on her hips. "Aren't you guys supposed to obey *me*? I thought I was the bride."

"Hilarious, considering the incentive we had to provide to get you to make choices." Gunner smirks as he flips the pages in the magazine.

Sophie shoots him a dirty look before Roman turns her chin. He arches an eyebrow, and she bites her lip. "You get incentive too. Or to provide it, or however, it works."

He nods and kisses her temple. "Give me something to do, Bambina."

"You can make me come." She offers.

Roman rolls his eyes, but I see the hint of a smile on his lips. Sophie is one in a million because no one can break Roman's bad moods that quickly. He sits down with us and we explain what we have going on.

Roman picks up some magazines and looks at the designs, looks at the venue we selected, and nods, glad that it's suitable no matter the weather–as predicted. Then he goes through the décor.

We look at several things, and talk as Sophie sits on Roman's lap, working on the guest list. When Holden finishes his, he hands it over and Sophie keeps adding, crossing out names as she goes.

Once we get done with the guest lists, other than Roman, who continues whispering things in Sophie's ear, we plate dinner.

Sophie looks exhausted, and I know it's not from the sex earlier. I think it's the stress. We've made huge amounts of progress, but we still have to check out some vendors, find someone to make the RSVP letters, send them out–which means getting addresses–and … well, everything else.

No one said planning a wedding would be easy.

"You should take some time off," Gunner murmurs, before stuffing his face with food.

Sophie looks up at him and Roman wraps an arm around her waist as if it's necessary to keep her in place. She looks around the table, taking us all in. I was thinking about it earlier, but I didn't dare say it. I wouldn't suggest that when she's already had so many questions about whether she wants to work.

She chews her lip and shakes her head. "No. I have to save up my time off for the wedding."

"It's just so much to accomplish, even more intense when you only have weekends to meet with vendors and test things, look at things, and so on."

"We can do some things on our time," Roman insists. "This isn't just Sophie's wedding. It's ours too. I can always double-check flower arrangements and take care of that."

"I can handle the baker, at least get the ball rolling, so all you have to worry about is the tasting," Gunner says.

"And I can handle getting the addresses for all our guests." Holden shrugs. "Should be easy enough and I can do that between work things, or while waiting for things to be shipped."

Sophie looks between us and relaxes. I reach over and take her hand. "We're all in this together, sweetheart. All we need is to make a plan."

"And keep to it," she says. "Which means one of you needs to make sure that I don't distract every meeting."

"I'm more than happy to tell you no," I say. "Like right now. Sophie, we're making progress. Save all those ideas for later."

She still wiggles against Roman until he grabs her hips. "Easy. I'm trying to be worried."

"Not allowed." She wraps her free arm around the back of his neck. "No worry zone."

"My family will not understand what's going on. I'll have to explain it to them. I may need to take some time before the wedding to talk to them."

"Massimo is going to lose his mind." Gunner chuckles.

That starts a whole round of conversation that's getting more heated. Sophie gets off of Roman and glares at him.

"If your grandmother calls me *that*, I will not talk to her at all."

I need to get better at Italian. Roman shrugs. "I don't know how she's going to take it. I want you to prepare for the worst."

"Then she's a, maybe."

"Sophie, I want my grandmother there."

"And I don't want to be called a whore at my wedding!" she yells. "If that's how she's going to behave, she's not welcome. I'm serious."

Roman says nothing to that, but then exhales. Sophie goes to the balcony and I pat his shoulder. "I got this."

As if I know what I'm going to say or do to fix this. I walk behind Sophie and rub her sides. "Talk to me."

"I didn't think about that. This is so … outside of what most people are comfortable with. What if they whisper just like Roman's grandma might? What if they say things or make comments? Maybe it should only be family."

"We want to let the people we care about know that we're in love," I whisper in her ear. "And if anyone says a bad word about you … Gunner's not the only one known to fight."

"Great. Fighting at a wedding." She huffs as her shoulders slump.

"If you focus on the worst, that's what we're going to get. The important part is us, sweetheart. We love you and we want you to be happy, to enjoy every moment of our wedding, just like we will."

She says nothing. She exhales and squirms in my arms. I tighten my arms around her, hugging her. "I've already started on my vows. I love you so much, Soph. If you don't want to go through with this, we're not too far along. You can say this is too soon, that we haven't prepared enough, but ..."

"But I don't want to cave to what other people want just because they don't understand what we're doing or who we are. It's not their fucking business. I just ... I don't want any fighting and I don't want to be worried that people are going to say things to me because I'm marrying all four of you."

And that's something I won't even touch. Before we had the sit-down conversation, I had resigned myself to accepting that Sophie would marry Gunner or Roman. Only because I've been comfortable with what we have, and I know Holden has, too. Neither of us had marriage on our bingo card for life.

But now that I get to give my vows, get to marry her, even in spirit, it's worth more than I thought it could be. I don't want to just stand to the side like a groomsman when I'm equal to Roman.

"I love you all. You know that. There's just so much. I'm already so stressed and next to nothing bad has come up. How am I going to handle all this planning in just six weeks? Things always come up and we don't have enough time to allow that to happen."

"And if you keep focusing on the bad things that *might* happen, you're going to get overwhelmed. So we're going to make sure you stay focused on what is. Let's limit the wedding stuff to only an hour and a half a day, okay? Except for weekends."

"Oh good, weekends." She rubs my hands. "Those things I used to like."

I chuckle. "And you think we're going to keep our hands off you with all this romance in the air? We'll reward you for every step forward, Sophie."

She slumps against me, then turns and hugs me. "It's been one week and I feel like I'm already …"

"Finish the thought."

"Like I already need counseling to keep my stress down." She rubs my chest. "Maybe that's another option? An hour a week of stress management. I think it might be helpful."

"Maybe."

Something buzzes and Sophie pulls out her phone. She groans. "Okay. I have to do the planning that you guys aren't allowed to see. Valerie will be coming up this weekend and dress shopping is a thing that's going to happen."

"Which is four whole days away. Do what you need to do and trust us to take care of some things, too."

"You guys decorated this place and set up the best proposal possible," Sophie agrees. "I suppose I can allow you to make plenty of choices."

"And we'll make sure we agree with each other. We're not terrible at cooperation." I wink.

With that, she grabs an armful of magazines and goes to her room. Of course, as we go further and further, and then look at the list, my promise of compromise and reasoning is close to an end.

Gunner doesn't want Holden's mom showing up since she's judgmental. Holden doesn't want any of Gunner's exes showing and we're all divided between having Matthew and Bella show. The only thing we've agreed on is that no one from work other than us and Miles.

When I get into bed, my mind is racing. I stare at my ceiling and shake my head. Weddings are always beautiful and look so easy from the outside. Maybe I should talk to Matthew about what he and Bella did to get things finished and get things moved forward in a better way.

But we have less than six weeks. Honestly, we have about four to get most of these things solidified. I don't want to pile onto Sophie. I want to help as much as I can, but we all have full-time jobs, and I feel that Sophie's right about things popping up when we need them the least.

We'll need to schedule the cake tasting–something we all need to go to–on a Sunday, if that's possible, making it convenient for all of us to get there. Which means trusting Gunner to do something and not putting it off because he'd rather do something else.

And we'd all rather do Sophie.

Just before I go to sleep, I feel my bed move and turn to see Sophie. She has on one of Roman's shirts, so I'm sure he got some attention from her, but she crawls into bed with me and snuggles close.

I wrap my arm around her and kiss her forehead. "It's okay, sweetheart."

"Tell me more logical things?"

"Are you overthinking in bed all by yourself?"

"Yes. Not even sex helped." She rubs my chest. "But I'm willing to give it another try for you."

I chuckle and kiss her softly. "Let's call it stress relief."

SOPHIE

Even with all the wedding planning taking place, I enjoy being able to rely on my men for stress relief. Nick started us using that to talk about it, but I like it. It's still fun, and it's keeping our passion alive, but by Saturday, having taken multiple work breaks with Holden and Roman, since he worked from home one day, and spending the night with Gunner and Nick until my brain turned off each time, I still feel the weight of every choice on my shoulder.

The guys have left me loving and silly notes when they give me things to look over. I know they're working so hard to keep me from being upset, but I just can't shake it.

I adjust in Roman's arms and he grunts, trying to reclaim me even as I reach for my phone. Five minutes until my alarm goes off to head to my mom's.

"Who says you're allowed to leave?" he asks.

"My schedule," I say. "It's not by choice."

He swats my bottom. "I'm going to remind you every day how much I appreciate you."

"By spanking me?"

"Yes." He chuckles against the back of my shoulder. "Among other ways."

"I'm sorry for yelling at you about your grandma. I like her. I just hate the idea of people judging. I can't believe I've agreed to Bella and Matthew coming after everything at their wedding. And then inviting some close college friends."

"The invitations go out today. You pulled five people–used all your vetoes."

"Don't remind me," I say. "Damn Gunner and his exes."

Roman chuckles and I feel it seep through my body and loosen my muscles. He rubs over my hip and strokes just above my pussy. I groan and shake my head. "I have to leave in five minutes."

"I can work with that." He nibbles my throat. "I bet I can make you come in three."

"Roman," I pant. "Please."

"Alright. Then cuddle me until the alarm goes off."

I roll and hug him. He's all sexy and soft after sleep. His hair is a mess and his eyes are gentle. I snuggle closer to him and nuzzle his neck. He feels good, warm, and safe.

If it was possible, I'd cuddle all my guys at once. That sounds excellent. A comfortable pile, like I'm a dragon hoarding the sexiest men in the world. I smile and Roman nudges me, wanting to know what I'm thinking.

We end up talking and teasing each other in those five minutes. Roman even pulls the blanket over our heads like we're little kids, sharing secrets when we're supposed to be asleep. When my alarm goes off, he covers my ears.

"You hear nothing."

"What?!" I yell.

He pulls his hands off my ears and I gasp. "My alarm!"

Narrowing his eyes, he shakes his head. "You tricked me."

"Only because I love you." I kiss him, then get up and change. Before I leave, I kiss all my guys goodbye. We need to go on a date.

I decide that as I head to my parents' place. We are overdue and I think we need the *actual* stress relief. Beyond sex, we need to go out and not think about the wedding. We can just hang out and not be bothered by all the looming deadlines.

But, considering I have an entire side-bag full of decisions to show my mom, maybe we can knock out some items on the never-ending, ever-growing list of things to do.

Fingers crossed.

As soon as I get to my mom's, she sweeps me inside and gives me a whole notebook full of things to consider. I show her the invitation list–complete with no room for changes–and then show her the venue for the reception, show off the colors we've decided on based on the garden, some of the other decisions, our plans, and our appointments.

"Well, I see a lot taken care of." She nods. "Good. Today we'll get you set with a dress, then we need to figure out when you can get the guys to practice dancing with you for your first dance, pick out those songs, and choose the songs for each of the guys to dance with their mothers, the song for you and your father, and if you want any games at the reception."

She keeps talking and instead of focusing on her words, I'm just counting the sentences before she takes a breath. Ten. Ten complete sentences without a breath.

When she takes one, I look at my watch. "Isn't Valerie ..."

"Here!" She comes in through the door. "I arrived early, so I got a taxi. I'm so ready for dress shopping. I got the yes and no signs and I'm so pumped to be extra judgey and detail-focused! Put me to work!"

And there's no arguing with them. Not when they sweep me into a limo and start pouring champagne. Thank god for champagne. By the time we get to the shop—even though it feels more like a mansion for a bunch of dresses—I don't mind much of anything.

I'm nice and relaxed, ready to try on everything and anything.

Until I see the dresses, my mom has laid out and see that Valerie is pulling out more. Dear god. This is going to be so much longer than it will take me to come down from my buzz. I start with the ones I know are going to be a no.

I hate the poofy princess dresses. I don't want to be kept so far from my men. Once I rule those out, I look at A-lines, then see the mermaid cut. I like the way it fits my hips; I like that I can still move in it, and if we adjust the bottom, it will trail behind me.

And I like the lace.

My mom and Valerie agree on that style of skirt, which means we're now focusing on tops. Which also means trying different textures. I don't want it to be too busy, since we're going to be in a garden for the ceremony and I'm sure I want the option to pin the back so I can dance without stepping on my dress.

After no less than ten dresses, I ask for a break.

I call Gunner and sigh. He chuckles. "Having fun, Sweets?"

"Tell me a joke or something."

"I've been offered three dates by gay men at this bakery. I think that the maintenance guy slipped his number in my ass pocket."

"That's my favorite pocket," I grumble.

"Don't worry. I'm still all about you and Roman."

It works. I smile. The guys have learned that flirting with Roman and seeing his face redden because he's not sure what to say makes me laugh. They've even been turning it on each other, trying to outdo each other and see who caves first.

I close my eyes and take a slow breath. "Can't I just show up naked?"

"Don't tempt me," he groans. "You could show up in just flowers and I'd be happy. Plus, it would give us a schedule to stay on so we can ravish you later."

Two knocks on the door tell me I have to get back out there. "Thank you, Gun. I love you."

"I'm serious, woman!"

But I hang up and roll my eyes. The woman brings in a dress and hangs it up. When I see the huge amount of fabric, I arch my eyebrow, but she holds up her hands. "Your mom told me you're getting married in a garden and that you light up like a fairytale princess whenever you talk about your ... husbands. Plural–is that right?"

I nod.

She smiles and motions to the dress. "I know you said you didn't want the princess style, but this one isn't as full in the skirt, and I think you will like it. It's a unique dress for your unique wedding."

I sigh and try it on. I stare at myself in the mirror. It's not what I had in mind, but ... I kind of love it. Almost clear fabric anchors the dress over my shoulder and shows a plunging neckline that almost shows my belly, but the dress is ... like a dream.

The ruffles of white fabric keep it from looking slutty and instead make it magical. The pretend sleeves fall over my arms and brush my forearms with their delicate lace and then the skirt, it's layered fabric, but is light, airy, and sweeps around me making me feel small and still powerful somehow.

"Wow," I breathe.

She clasps her hands as she finishes pulling it in the back. "You look like a princess, but the kind that saves herself."

I walk out in the dress and I see Valerie's jaw hit the floor. My mom tears up and clasps her hands together under her chin. The woman puts my hair in a low bun, then sets a veil in my bun, so it doesn't cover the front of the dress and my eyes water.

I love it. A dress I never would have chosen, but wow. Just … wow. I can see myself in the garden, standing out from the color and the art. I can wear whatever necklace I want, it has so many options and all I can think is: yes.

"So, Mom, Maid of Honor, what do you think?"

"If you don't choose this dress, I'm done with you." Valerie threatens. "It's the first one that's given you that dreamy look in your eyes."

"This is it," I say. "This is the dress. The only one that could … That could be enough."

My mom bounces. "Oh my god, yes. Just yes. Your dad is going to have a cow, then he's going to cry. I can already see the pictures."

"It's an Elihav Sasson. A good pick, I think. Especially for the venue." The saleswoman continues.

I nod and stroke over the skirt. "It's perfect."

It's so perfect that I don't want to take it off. I want to live in it, to wear it, to bask in the fact that I'm getting married. We clink champagne glasses together and I hug my mom and my best friend as we all cry.

"I feel like a bride." I blubber. "It's the first time."

"And don't you worry about anything else," Valerie says. "Your mom and I are going to make sure everything else goes to plan. All you have to do is choose and we'll be on the vendors like crazy."

I laugh and wipe my eyes. I can't believe I have a dress. I spin in it and Valerie dips me back, so I can see myself in the mirror.

There are still a million and a half things to stress about, but seeing this, posing for a picture with Valerie, then my mother as they start talking alterations makes it real.

In five weeks, I'm getting married. The four men I love will be mine forever. All mine and a whole day will be about our relationship, celebrating what we've built together while setting a high bar for our future.

We're going to get there. We'll be at the altar, we'll say the vows, we'll dance, we'll drink, we'll have everything we've ever wanted, including the fairytale of happily ever after.

When I take off the dress and say goodbye, for now, a weight leaves my chest. That's what's important. None of the other details matter–I was right at the beginning. As long as I have my men waiting for me at the end of the aisle and they get as misty-eyed by my dress and me as my mom did, then everything will be right with the world.

We can make it there. We will.

ROMAN

"A photographer," I say. "We don't have one yet."

Massimo hums in his throat as he pours Gunner, Nick, Holden, and me another glass of bourbon. Gunner looks around the twenties-themed speakeasy and sighs. "I took Sophie here once."

"Not on subject." Mass nudges him. "But I want to hear all about that later."

Gunner winks and shoots Massimo a set of finger guns which makes me roll my eyes. Nick looks at the list we have. "Okay, So Sophie is handing everything we've decided on over to her mother and Valerie to follow through on. The big thing right now is the cake and the flowers."

"You know, if any of the vendors give you trouble, you should sic Danny on them." Massimo gets that loving look in his eyes. "Even since we had the baby, she's a hellcat."

"Too much information," I murmur in Italian.

"She could make someone obedient with her stern voice and that coach-level glare. You know she can bring men twice her size to heel, right? She's a goddess." He continues anyway.

"How did you plan everything and get it done in time?" Nick asks him.

"We had a year. My Tesoro was a battle to get to the alter. The baby-making part was easier." Massimo chuckles. "It's good you guys are doing it in the right order. Grandma gave me hell for having a bastard, her words." He takes a long drink.

I roll my eyes, but grandma is my biggest worry. Mom knows that I've always been unconventional and I think she's just relieved I'm getting married instead of living the bachelor life forever. Every year she's made sure that I don't have a child of my own running around without a father.

"Roman." Gunner nudges me. "Sophie is worked up today. Let's get as much done as we can, okay?"

"The cake tasting tomorrow will help," I assure him. "Sweets seem to help with stress."

Holden smirks and I see Nick do the same. As much stress as we've been under, we've found the best way to deal with it. Sex is an incentive, a way to relax, and most importantly, in those moments right after I finish, everything is clear.

It's so easy to get lost in the details, in every little thing that we have to make sure doesn't go wrong, to focus on the chairs or the plates instead of the reason this is happening. We love Sophie. Love cuddling her, touching her, kissing her, and losing ourselves in her is a reminder we need considering the mad dash we're making to the alter.

"Dress shopping?" Massimo guesses, replying to me when no one else does.

We all nod and he hisses. "The hardest part for the bride."

"Not Sophie." Nick seems sure of that as he finishes his drink. "With her Mom and Valerie there, I bet they're close to done if not already out doing something different."

"Did you guys decide if kids are allowed or not?"

"Of course they are." Holden looks around the table like he can't believe anything else would be an option.

"I'm just saying, some people have a no-kids wedding. I don't get it, but it's kind of important considering the baby." Mass shrugs.

"Cigars are necessary. We never celebrated that." Nick decides, getting up.

Holden goes with him so they can keep talking about how they're dealing with the hotel and booking rooms in a block so our guests can be together and we can be sure to only cover people for the wedding.

I rub my forehead. There's so much to do. The cake tasting should be the last big thing other than getting over there, but Sophie will lose it if we don't have a photographer. I drink to calm my stomach. How is it possible to get through all this?

"I still can't believe you got her father's permission. Four men? For marriages?" Mass shakes his head. "Must be a rare breed. Especially since he's your friend."

"There's a deal in place," I murmur. "If we get into even one fight that threatens the marriage, his support is gone."

"Ouch."

"It can't be that hard." Gunner shrugs, refilling his glass. "We're managing it right now. Sex, choices, more sex, firm decisions, work, food, and sex. It's working."

"Get back to me at the two-week mark. That's when shit starts to hit the fan. Danny and I fought before, but nothing like that," Massimo murmurs, but before he drinks he pauses as his brow furrows. "It could have been the pregnancy hormones too."

"We're taking care of as much as possible," I say. "We're spreading responsibilities and making sure that Sophie has everything she needs."

"Stress is stress." Massimo shrugs. "You know that, Roman."

Despite getting plenty done, I know he's right. When we get home, Nick reminds us Sophie might not be in the best mood. "Her mom was insistent they wouldn't leave until she found a dress."

"And she called me begging for a joke," Gunner says.

"So if she's home, she might not be the happiest. Roman, that means you may be needed in the kitchen." Holden nods. "I grabbed some flowers for her."

"I can ... take off my shirt." Gunner gives a drunken smile. "Always makes her smile."

I roll my eyes and open the door to see Sophie talking with Valerie. They look at something on her phone before Valerie takes it and shoves it in her bra. Sophie jumps up and beams at us.

"My wonderful grooms are home!"

Yup, they've been in the wine. When Sophie kisses me, I can taste it on her lips. I kiss her, still frustrated I didn't get the make-out session I was hoping for this morning. I cup her face in my hands and see a starry look in her eyes that has been gone since we jumped into planning mode.

"Are you happy, Bambina?"

"Yes," she hums. "Amore."

I groan at the Italian and kiss her again. I will not be able to control myself if she keeps this up. Making me feel special and loved in my language. She twirls under my arm and kisses Gunner next.

He licks his bottom lip. "You're my favorite flavor—alcohol."

She giggles and rubs his chest. "So are you."

Then on to Nick. She whispers something in his ear and he rubs her hip. "Yes, sweetheart."

Holden shows Sophie the flowers, and she pulls one out and puts it behind his ear before kissing him. Valerie giggles, "You guys are so whipped."

"Oh no. That's Sophie you're talking about." Gunner tosses her over his shoulder and swats her bottom. "And she always thanks us for that."

"I do not!" She yells.

I hear her patting Gunner's butt and she giggles. "We should make a blanket fort and get all cozy."

"Listen, I came here to escape the nausea-inducing cuteness that is your parents." Valerie gives Sophie a wedgie while she can't do anything about it, making Gunner nearly drop her. "I'm not putting up with it here too."

But I get to work in the kitchen and soon enough find an apron being tied around my neck and waist. Sophie kisses my shoulder. "I love you, Roman."

"I love you too, Soph." I kiss her temple. "No more wine."

"Nope. Can't stain my teeth with the wedding coming up." Then she looks around. "Is Massimo coming for dinner?"

"He is."

"Good." She smiles and when I squirm, she scratches the itchy spot on my back until I moan. "He deserves a little break from the baby."

"I think he misses it already," I say. "He keeps looking at his phone and demanding videos and pictures."

Sophie smiles and hugs me again. "Do you want babies?"

I blink a few times. I know we're doing the marriage thing, but that's separate from the baby thing. It shouldn't be. Honestly, we should have had this conversation before I ever proposed. I turn around, ignoring the pasta, even though my grandma would hit me for it.

"Do you want babies?"

"Maybe." She takes my hands with hers. "I think it could be fun. Not right away though. I haven't had enough baby-free fun with you guys."

"Oh, sounds like you want to do dangerous things," I tease.

"I do! I want to go cage diving with great white sharks. I want to travel. I want to get a tattoo maybe or go on a vacation with you guys where we don't need a babysitter or a kids area. I can wait a year or … three for the sleepless nights, the long car rides, and the terrible twos."

"But you want them?" Nick asks.

"I think I do." She nods.

"No baby talk!" Valerie yells from the couch where she's doing research on something. "*First* comes marriage. That means after the wedding you can start talking babies."

Holden chuckles and looks over Valerie's shoulder. They start talking about something relating to PTSD and I glance at Sophie as if trying to tell her that may not be the best conversation. But instead, she's pulling Gunner up behind her so she's sandwiched between us.

"I like this position." She keeps her voice low in that tempting little whisper that tends to get her whatever she could want. "We should put it to use soon."

"Naughty girl," Gunner teases. "Who said I want your cooties?"

She gasps. "I don't have cooties!"

"Who knows? You spent all day playing dress-up. Sounds like the kind of thing that is infectious."

"Says the guy who only has to try on suits and ties."

"Impossible to handle. What if they are different shades of black!" Gunner gasps.

"Then the world will implode because everyone will notice. Even the flowers will judge." She giggles. "Can you imagine?"

Gunner rolls his eyes. "Keep this up and I'm not painting your toenails tonight."

She pouts. "But you promised!"

He shrugs. "Sarcasm isn't nice."

"For adults it is." She looks to me for help. "Tell him."

"If she wasn't half this sassy, you wouldn't love her as much," I say.

Gunner sighs and squeezes her cheeks together, so she looks like a chipmunk. "It's true. I love how much you challenge me and that we can sass each other without feelings getting hurt."

"I love you," she says.

"What? That didn't sound like sarcasm. I'm not fluent in normal English," Gunner says.

Sophie shoves him and laughs.

I feel a smile curl up my cheeks. We walked in expecting her to be exhausted, annoyed, at her wit's end, and holding on. Instead, we get to see the Sophie we fell in love with. Not the one so thoroughly rattled by stress that she can barely function without losing her temper.

When I finish cooking, someone knocks and Sophie lets Massimo in. He picks her up in a crushing hug and then pats her head.

"Look at you, about to steal my cousin away." He smiles at her.

She answers him in Italian, determined to practice. "We'll be happy forever."

Massimo beams and spins her around. "Such good Italian on you! Grandma will be pleased."

"If she doesn't get upset about the whole multiple husband thing." There's that frustrated edge again.

The fight I'm most worried about: how others are going to be a problem at the wedding. Luckily, I'm heading to Italy before we get married to make sure it's clear that Sophie is marrying all four of us.

If Grandma doesn't like it, she doesn't have to be there. It will break my heart, but it's not just my heart in question. Sophia is just as important and she deserves to be happy, not worried about people judging.

Now if I can make myself believe that and remind myself daily that compromise will give us a happy day to start the rest of our life on, we won't have a problem.

SOPHIE

*D*inner is amazing. As it always is when Roman cooks. Valerie moans. "Okay, I get why you're marrying the big quiet one."

I choke on the spaghetti at her comment. She pats my back, and Gunner narrows his eyes at Valerie. "Look, Val, you're sweet and all, but you can't start poisoning her to steal her husbands until after the marriage."

"As if I want your alcohol-soaked butt." She laughs.

"Oh, it's not my butt you said you wanted when we were at the strip club," he says, pointing his fork at her.

Valerie narrows her eyes. I remember her saying she wanted to see if his dick was big enough to make her like him, then going for his buttons before I got in the way and told her that consent is still a thing.

So she turned her eyes on the strippers, rubbing asses, slipping ones, and cheering for the pole dancers. Gunner grins as the silence continues, promising him victory. But then Valerie kisses my neck.

"Should we tell them about that one time in college?"

It's my turn to go red as I shake my head and put a roll in her mouth. "No."

It was a party. Truth or dare and my first girl-on-girl experience. We'd gotten put together for seven minutes of heaven, and we gave it the college try. We didn't go all the way, hell we didn't even take off our clothes, but our hands wandered as we made out.

But Gunner would beg for details and that would make me lose my mind. With everything else in my current balancing act, I don't need my guys wondering about my sexuality. I clear my throat. "So the cake tasting tomorrow?"

Holden arches an eyebrow. "Now I'm curious."

"I am too." I continue. "About the different flavors. What do you think we can expect, Gunner?"

"More of you avoiding what is going to be a great story." He smirks. "I think Val has something fun to share."

"Maybe I'll save it for my maid of honor speech."

Just like that, my face pales. Oh god. Speeches. I forgot all about that. At some weddings, it's just the parents of the couple, the maid of honor, and the best man. I don't even know who the best man is. If it's my dad, and he's drunk … oh god.

I sit back from my food, not caring that there's still half a plate there. If Dad doesn't approve, he'll make it clear with the speech. My mom is going to be inappropriate as usual. Which means even if we get Roman's grandma and all the other families on board, my parents can ruin it within two minutes or less.

"Soph, I'm kidding." Valerie rubs my back. "I will not embarrass you, I promise. I know how hard the day is going to be when it comes to family stuff."

"Who's the best man?" I look between my guys.

They look at one another, then all of them look at Massimo. He beams. "I was nominated by popular vote."

"To be fair, I think he's the only one that's close to all of us other than Matthew and your dad." Holden shrugs.

"Close and like." Gunner clarifies. "And If Matthew is involved in the wedding, Bella might want to be too and we can't have that."

I nod and rub the back of my neck. "Speeches."

"Are a thing."

"We are only going to allow these two to talk." I motion to Valerie and Massimo. "I don't trust my dad and definitely don't trust my mom."

"But she's so much fun," Nick teases. "Makes me feel young and sexy." He winks.

"I do that nightly." I point at him.

He chuckles and Massimo laughs and chokes. Roman hits his back once, and he coughs up his food, then continues eating like nothing happened. Of course.

Dinner continues, but by the time we're done, I've been refilled with worries. Even as I lie in bed with Valerie, I just keep thinking.

The cake tasting tomorrow will go well, but we all have to agree on four flavors out of I don't know how many. Maybe I should just let the guys choose–give them total control over something. Or everything at this point.

I have my dress. What other decision do I need to make?

And Nick has already started on his vows–lucky him–and I have four still to write. Valerie snores and flops over as I get up and stare at my notebook. I've started one for each of them, but other than a blanket "I love you" I do not know what to write.

Some brides said it just came to them and they could move forward with it and get everything set the night before.

But those brides only had one man. I have four. I can't procrastinate.

And knowing I can't procrastinate adds enough pressure to make me want to. Because it should be easy. I've been romantic with them plenty of times over, but I just can't make it happen.

And I have songs to choose.

How am I even able to take time to sleep? Not to mention the emails that have been piling up for work that I'm going to have to deal with on Monday. I take a few deep breaths, then go to the balcony.

It's easier to breathe here. I can stare down at the city and the people look like ants. Central park is dark and … almost welcoming. Because when I'm here, my name doesn't matter. The day of the week doesn't matter, nothing matters at all. I'm no one to the city.

Exhaling, I rub my temples. The vows will come.

They will. I know I love these men. I know that in the morning, I'll still love them. Even through all this stress, they're worth it. I know it. Even if my words end up being clumsy, they'll be real.

The cake tasting will go fine. I can listen to romantic songs and find one for each of them. It will all be fine.

And if I keep saying that, my head might believe it. I can just accept that I'm allowed to be happy and there doesn't have to be a cost for it. Even though this happily ever after seems like it shouldn't exist.

Things never go this well, which means there's some problem lurking around some corner and I don't even know how to prepare for it. My phone buzzes and I see a text from Holden that's telling me to go to bed.

I roll my eyes and look over my shoulder. He smirks at me and joins me outside on the balcony. "Sleep deprivation only makes stress worse, baby."

"Is that why my head is trying to find issues?" I ask.

"Maybe. What's wrong?"

"There's just so much. I feel like we've already made a million choices. I mean, I picked my dress today. We're picking cake tomorrow and so much is already taken care of, but there's so much more to do."

"Like what?"

"I have to make the rest of my bridal party. Pick out songs for our first dances. We should go and take lessons for dancing. Plus the vows. And the father-daughter dance. All you guys dancing with your moms."

"My mom isn't coming," he murmurs.

I freeze, then meet his eyes. "Holden ... why?"

"She hasn't been a part of my life since I went into the military. She hated it. It scared her, I think. We haven't talked in a very long time."

"But ... but if she loves you-"

"She's also very traditional, Sophie. There is nothing about this wedding she'd support. I don't want her there. I'd rather avoid it all together. Her not being there won't bother me. In fact, it would be weirder if she was there."

It's sad. Horribly sad that they haven't talked, that she doesn't want to be in his life, that she's missing out on everything. Holden smiles and kisses my forehead. "It's my choice, Sophie. Also, I think choosing the song to dance with you should be my choice too."

"Holden."

"You can approve it. I'll give you three options. How about that?" he asks. "Compromise."

"I've heard it helps with things," I grumble.

Holden hugs me, his arms winding tight and making me feel safe and sane. He kisses me again and then grabs my bottom. "You should get to bed before my libido acts up."

"Oh, you want to fuck me on the balcony now?" I tease.

"Well, I fucked you on the roof with the guys. The balcony sounds like a pretty good place to do it. Wake up the entire city, make you forget about all this worry," he whispers in my ear, low and breathy.

A shiver teases my spine, but before I can form an answer, Holden already has me inside and is walking me to my room. "But you have a guest, so I'll behave."

"For tonight?"

"Just tonight." He winks at me. "And because we have to be up early."

"Prepare for cake."

His face looks a little green. "I'm not the biggest fan of sweets. I can't promise I'm going to try everything."

"That's okay." I kiss him. "I love you."

"And that's all the sweetness I need," he hums.

Somehow, I get sleep. But as soon as my alarm goes off, it's go-go-go. There's no stopping productivity. I end up dressed, and turned around twice because I keep forgetting things, but once we're in the limo, there's no turning around. I keep wondering what else I've forgotten because there has to be something, but Gunner takes my hand.

"Stop worrying. Just accept today. Okay? After cake, we can go to some bodega and get some salty, unhealthy treats and relax. We've earned it."

"How do we have time to relax?"

"Because I say so, and I'm in charge." He shrugs, then flashes a wide smile when I narrow my eyes. "And because if you're a good girl, I get to reward you."

"You couldn't keep your hands off me either way. Where's the incentive?"

"The amount of times you get to come is the incentive, Sweets," he purrs in my ear. "One or five. It's up to you?"

I squirm and squeeze my thighs together. He's got a hell of a point there. I do like coming and with that number, I'm thinking it might be a group session which I would love. I love having them separately and being able to focus all my attention on one man at a time, but having all of them touch me, overwhelm me, and turn me into a quivering mess of pleasure is long overdue.

By the time we get to the bakery, I'm more than happy to behave, state my opinion, and move on. Especially if that means getting to have more fun with my men. But then we're seated around an enormous table and I see little sample cakes spread out.

The chef has a pink stripe running through his hair and claps his hands together. "So, we have several flavors for you all to try. There is vanilla, lemon, devil's chocolate and chocolate ganache. There is also an almond and orange cake, butterscotch, and–my favorite–a mascarpone cake with strawberries."

We each get a little bit of it, with the frosting to try. I try the mascarpone first and fall in love. It's light and fluffy with just the right amount of sweetness. The ripeness of the strawberries is even better. I end up eating the entire piece.

Gunner nudges me. "Am I going to roll you out of here?"

"Maybe, but I'll be fat and happy," I tease him back.

"Sounds like the best possible scenario."

GUNNER

*H*oly fuck, the cake is amazing. The Devil's chocolate is sinful and I swear I'm ready to claim it all as mine. Sophie takes one bite of the butterscotch and freezes, schooling her expression. I choke as I steal a bite from her plate.

It's sweet. She shakes her head and then says she's done. She lets the others finish and then her hand brushes my thigh. I guide her to my cock and she rubs the spot until I'm hard and eager to pull her hand into my jeans so she can take full advantage of what I have to offer.

But a throat is cleared and I get a harsh look from Valerie. Just to get under her skin, I rub my hand along the inside of Sophie's thigh until I'm teasing her underwear … except she's not wearing any, and she jumps a little when my finger brushes her slit.

Her face goes bright red and I see Holden smirk. Roman's eyes flick to hers and the desire there is so hot that I know she's not getting away tonight without dealing with all four of us.

"So, the decisions." Valerie tries to refocus.

Massimo keeps grinning to himself as he shoves the rest of his cake down his throat. The man acts like he's never fed, although I know he eats more than anyone else alive.

"I love the mascarpone," Sophie says to fill the silence as she pushes my hand away from her pussy.

"The devil's cake is my top." I tighten her hand around my cock when she tries to pull it away.

"The mascarpone won me over too," Holden agrees. "But I liked the vanilla as well and I think it would be good to have that for guests."

"I liked the Devil's chocolate, even if it means agreeing with that asshole." Valerie glares at me. "But the orange almond. Heavenly." She closes her eyes and licks her finger.

"Agreed." Nick sighs. "It was so light and perfect. A good balance of sweet."

Roman looks between the flavors and nods. "I enjoyed the Vanilla and the orange almond."

"All were amazing. I will take the leftovers," Massimo says.

Sophie laughs until I grind against her hand. Her eyes go to me and she sucks in a harsh breath. I smirk. "So, what's the verdict?"

"Vanilla, mascarpone, orange almond, and the devil's chocolate." Her low voice, the rough edge to it, makes my cock twitch.

"Calm down over there," Valerie orders.

My friend tries to hide his smirk behind his hand before he nods. "Four tiers, one of each."

"And six cupcakes of each, just to make sure we have enough," Nick decides. "If there are any leftover, we know who will take them."

"Hell yes! I love being the best man," Massimo shouts.

We all laugh, then go to a little hole-in-the-wall shop for lunch. A nice Cuban place I swear by. Valerie sits between me and Sophie and narrows her eyes. "If you're marrying my best friend for the sex and only the sex, I will cut your dick off."

"Sex wouldn't get her a ring." I hiss. "Just because I'm very happy to show her how much she turns me on doesn't mean that's the reason I love her."

"Then how about you tell me why."

"How about you wait until I say my vows," I say. "You already gave your approval."

"I'm waiting," she says.

I groan. "Fuck, I love her, Valerie. I love that she encourages me. I love how she looks at me and makes me feel. I love how she refuses to take opportunities to get ahead that she didn't earn. I love her determination and sass and the way she gets things done, no matter the odds. She accepts me for everything I am, even the shit I don't like showing. She never asks me to change or be something I'm not."

"So, other than your dick?"

"You didn't get to see that," I say. "And I don't appreciate you giving *me* hell rather than anyone else."

"You're the one always making the moves."

"So is Sophie," I say. "I do nothing without consent."

Valerie looks at Sophie, who's not at all pretending to be innocent considering how she's rubbing her ass against Holden while ordering, pretending to need to bend over to see the options better. Holden's face is drawn tight, trying to keep himself composed.

Valerie huffs, but I don't let her escape the question. "I'm serious. Why are you up my ass?"

"You set me up with three men when I didn't ask you to. You know Hunter has messaged me six times asking to go out?"

"Well, you kissed his brother." I shrug. "I didn't do that."

"You cornered me in to a situation with them. I don't appreciate being forced to do anything, Gunner, and you didn't *have* to do that. You chose to, based on one drunk comment."

"So you're telling me that if they're at the wedding and Leif asks you to dance, you'll say no?"

"Absolutely."

"Then let's place a bet. If any of them ask you to dance and you say yes, send me the best apology card they have."

She puts her hand in mine and the force of her fingers takes my breath away. She crushes my hand.

"Okay." She shrugs.

She releases me and I skirt around to the back of the line, nervous to be in her crosshairs. How the hell is Sophie friends with a take-no-shit woman like Valerie? She could be fucking president with that attitude. I bet she'd climb the ranks fast.

Is that why she's in DC? Laying the groundwork and spreading fear through any guy with a cock he wants to keep attached? It's a damn good political strategy. But of course, when she's with Sophie, it's all smiles and sweetness which makes me feel crazy.

I grumble to myself as I eat, and Holden nudges me. "Everything good?"

"Valerie is a pain in the ass," I say. "She thinks I'm not good enough for Sophie that I don't love her."

"Prove her wrong," Holden says. "Even Miles knows you love her. Just stop being an ass all the time when she's around and stop challenging her."

"My sweetness is saved for Sophie, for when she's alone and … and …"

"And you feel safe being vulnerable? Your vows can't all be jokes, Gun. Make small attempts now when it's just us. We are the wedding party, after all."

When we get back to the penthouse, I ask to talk to Sophie alone. She joins me on the balcony and I sit down rather than gluing myself to her like I want to. She turns, then sits next to me. "What's wrong, handsome?"

"You know I love you, right? Not just because of the sex."

"I know." She wraps my arm around her. "I like when we read together and when we talk about the power of fiction."

"There is power. It lets us experience a million different lives and learn where we can improve." I insist.

She giggles and kisses my cheek. "I like your playful side, your sweet side when you tell me things, even though I know you don't want to dig into some of them."

I take a deep breath. "Valerie doesn't like me."

"Nope." She shrugs. "Because she isn't willing to look deeper. You're a romantic at heart, Gunner. I know that."

I brush my thumb over her cheek. "You know, I think you're better than any woman I've ever read about. Even Elizabeth Bennett and she was always my favorite."

Sophie giggles and brushes her hand over mine, lacing our fingers. "That's a hell of a compliment."

"I like my women sassy and fierce. Which is part of why I love you so much. You never settled for only having me at surface level. You always wanted more."

"Because I know what an amazing man you are." She insists.

I lose myself in her eyes and shake my head. "You make me want to be a better man. You know that?"

"I know you've been drinking less and partying less. I know that as much as you tease me, come on to me, drive me crazy with lust, you'd be just as happy reading with me in the bath tub or watching a movie with me close by."

"Or destroying you in any board game?"

She giggles and kisses me. "I love you, Gunner. I don't care if my best friend doesn't know why. I don't care if no one understands why. I won't let you forget I do."

I sigh and kiss her softly. "If your vows are that good, I don't stand a fucking chance. I know I'm going to end up crying."

She hugs me and we sit like that for a while. "I have some ideas for poems for you and me. Do you want to look them over with me?"

"I'd love to. There are a few I'd like–nothing from the bible. Not between us." I kiss her forehead. "It's cliché, and nothing about us is."

Sophie lights up and kisses me like she alone can. My heart threatens to burst out of my chest to join hers. I rest my forehead against hers and dare for the cheesiest line I've ever read–in a book I never should have read. "So the lion fell in love with the lamb."

She cackles, laughs so hard her face goes red and I beam despite her knowing my secret. She shakes her head and laughs again. "Twilight?"

"That shit was romantic as hell the first time around. I swear."

She nuzzles my neck. "Well, you're my personal brand of heroin."

"You can't laugh like that when you've read it too," I grumble in response to her quote. "I promise to never watch you sleep by breaking in through a window."

"And I promise to read anything you recommend so I can keep getting to know you better," she whispers. "Even if it's ridiculous."

"That's a large list of books. Are you ready for that?"

"As ready as I am to marry you." She promises. "Are you ready for that?"

"My parents are coming and they're going to be a little surprised, but I've never been so ready to be with someone forever, Soph. When Bella was coming on to me in Hawaii, there wasn't even a tempted thought in my head. You destroyed other women for me. There's just you and I want the forever that only you can offer me."

She wipes at her eyes and shakes her head. "You can't do that to me."

"Oh, we're both screwed. We're going to be sobbing up there." I laugh, wiping at my eyes. "I can't wait."

She squeezes my hands. "Make me one more promise, okay?"

I hesitate, then nod.

"Promise me that no matter what is going on, you'll never stop talking to me like this? That you'll always be this open and sweet and good with me."

"That was already promised," I say. "When I proposed, I promised you me, as I am forever. That means all this soft gooey stuff, along with the kinky sex and the cuddling, and the adventures we go on."

"I'm all yours." She insists. Kissing me. She sucks my bottom lip, then draws back. "I have been for so long, Gun. You've never had a reason to worry."

"And I never will again ..." But I hesitate. "I might, but then we can have one of these pleasant conversations and fix it."

She leans against me and I glance over at the living room. I see Valerie watching, with her head turned to the side. Oh yeah, it's time to catch up, bestie. I know that even if Sophie says she doesn't care, it will mean the world to her if I can bond with Val, which means I'm going to find something in common with the hellion and make sure my future wife is happier than anyone–fiction or real life.

SOPHIE

*V*alerie gets on the plane in the morning and on the drive back I realize I don't miss her as much as the first or second time I dropped her off. Maybe it's because I know I'll see her again. Or maybe it's because now we're in more constant communication. It doesn't feel like there's as much space between New York and D.C.

But when I get home before I can get out of my car, I see a text from Roman saying he's going to be late tonight. I send a sad face and he sends me a heart in reply. I huff and go inside to see Holden waiting for me.

He bundles me up in his arms and kisses me. "How are you feeling about her leaving?"

"I don't *love* it, but it means sex is on the table again and I know I'll see her again soon." I sigh, pressing my head to his neck.

He smells so good. I know he uses one of the Old Spice soaps and the way it lingers on his skin is so delicious. I just want to keep hugging him. "You smell good."

But he doesn't laugh or do anything that I expect. He just rubs my back, which means there's bad news. I feel it like a current of electricity. "What is it, Hold?"

"Remember the asshole we told you about before? The one who likes to be involved, even though he's not a majority shareholder?"

"Yeah."

"He's back in town." Holden keeps petting me. "Apparently, some people have heard of our upcoming wedding and decided to drop in. To meet you."

"Eew," I mumble. "That puts a dent in to our available sex time."

Holden lifts my chin and his mouth molds to mine. I moan and tug on his shirt, wanting more. My fiancés have made me so greedy. Holden surrenders his shirt, letting me stroke over the planes of his chest and abs.

"Don't you try to seduce me, Miss Lane."

I laugh and kiss his neck. "Should I hyphenate my name? Four last names aren't too many."

He laughs this time, then kisses me again. "Whatever you want, baby. You have my ring, you have my heart, you don't need my last name but it's yours to have."

"How am I supposed to say something to that?" I ask, before standing on my toes and tugging him down to kiss me again.

"We were having a conversation," he says around my lips.

"Creepy guy wants to meet me," I summarize, still kissing him. "And I don't want to meet him."

"I don't know that we can avoid it." Holden keeps his mouth out of my reach.

I settle for kissing across his chest and rubbing his sides, tracing the V-cut that leads lower. "We could avoid this conversation and have fun before I start work."

He groans and holds my face in his hands. "Behave."

I pout.

"Just for this conversation, then you can ride my cock while I balance the books," he promises.

I bite my lip. "My goal will be to distract you."

"And you always succeed," he purrs against my mouth. "Always. But let's talk first."

I groan and give in. "I just don't want problems. That's all. And this sounds like a problem and I'm worried it's going to start a stress spiral."

"All you have to do is meet someone. That's all," Holden says. "Just a meeting and that's it."

I chew my lip and take a slow breath. It's another thing on my plate and I'm worried my plate is going to overflow. Sure, I've been removing stuff, but there are still the basics like figuring out the time off, getting over there, wanting to see Paris and still having to do all the work of finishing the wedding planning. I should have gotten a wedding planner.

"Talk to me," Holden says. "What's going on in that head?"

"A million things," I murmur. "Namely how much we have to do in the next few weeks to make sure everything is set. It's filling up and I feel like I'm going to crumble under the weight of it all."

"We are-"

I put my hand over his mouth. "Holden, I know all four of you are helping. And my mom and Valerie, but it still feels like there's too much to do for me to even sleep or enjoy time with you guys. Bella had so long to plan and get everything set and she was still so fucked up with stress that she tried to fuck Gunner."

He doesn't jump in which is nice, because, unlike my mom, I need to breathe while I talk. I calm the earthquake in my chest, threatening to split open and swallow my sanity and control.

"I'm hanging on, but I want to do more than hang on. I want to enjoy my time with you guys, not be bounced from thing to thing, and feel like I can't keep up. It scares me. That's my hesitation. That's all."

Then I nod. "Your turn."

Holden just hugs me until my worries seem to flee. His heartbeat is so strong, so calming. I exhale and Holden makes a soft sound. "There you go."

"Are your hugs magic?"

"Human heartbeats tend to sync. I can't hear yours, but since you can hear mine, it should help you calm down. I learned it in my first round of counseling," he murmurs. "Plus eight to ten positive touches a day make for better mental health."

"Full of knowledge, aren't you?" I feel my face heat.

"I have to be with you around." He kisses the top of my head. "If you feel overwhelmed, talking helps. It helps clear your mind. Other than fucking, which I'm more than happy to do as well."

"But now I can be focused on the sex and not every other thought in my head." I sigh, snuggling closer to him. "You're so reasonable. How am I supposed to be irrational and bitchy when you're so calm?"

"Let Gunner be bitchy for you." He suggests.

I kiss Holden's chest and nod. "I'll meet the asshole."

"I'm glad to hear it, baby."

We get through work, even with our sex break where Holden gives up almost immediately on trying to reconcile the books. By the time the end of the workday rolls around, I feel like I'm at least accomplished in one area.

Holden also shows me our to-do list. Roman got a photographer and the big things are taken care of. Until I notice something isn't on the list.

"Hold," I say.

He continues buttoning his shirt for dinner tonight and I tap him again. "Hold, we don't have wedding bands."

"What?" He looks at his hand.

"Those are engagement rings. Wedding bands are a thing. Maybe just one from all of you for me, with each of your names along the inside, but we need wedding bands to be married. It's part of it." I feel the stress rising in me, threatening to consume me as my lungs contract into my spine.

"Oh my god. It's so important. And the marriage certificate has to be done *before* the wedding, so we need to go to city hall. Fuck!"

"Hey."

"I knew something would fall through the cracks. I told you! I just should have quit as soon as you guys proposed. I should have insisted on a long engagement and-"

Holden kisses me, then, when I still try to talk, he changes the angle and kisses me again, deeper, his tongue soothing mine. Something perks my ears, but Holden strokes down my spine, then kisses me again.

Warmth against my back alerts me to someone else, but lips graze my neck and I shiver. Holden draws back and kisses my forehead. "I'm turning you over to Nick."

I'm spun and Nick kisses me hello. "Are you distracting Holden from getting dressed?"

"We forgot important things. I can't go to dinner. I have to contact city hall and find wedding bands and-"

"And that sounds like things that can wait until tomorrow considering city hall is closed right now." Nick pulls up my left hand and kisses my wrist. "And it wasn't forgotten. It's been prioritized. We have a master list, weekly lists, and 'maybe we'll get to it' lists."

"What lists? I haven't heard of them! I haven't even seen the master list!"

"You can." He kisses the inside of my elbow, then jerks me closer to press his lips to the hollow under my ear. "Tomorrow morning. I'll show you all of them."

I'm tempted to give in, but I shake my head. "We promised you guys wouldn't keep things from me anymore. Why haven't I seen these lists?"

Nick arches an eyebrow at my tone, but I don't care. We made a promise.

"I know we promised, Sophia."

"Then why do I have to repeat myself? I don't like that. It's a boundary I set so I wouldn't feel you guys are treating me like a kid. I'm not a kid. I'm going to be your wife and I want to feel respected and included and-"

"Your mother made them. She just tells us it's on the list when we ask and I asked her to send them to you more than a week ago." He continues watching me, frustrated and unhappy with my monologue.

I'm still angry. I can't just shake it off. "I don't want to go to this dinner."

"What *do* you want, then?"

"I want more time." Which I know isn't possible. "And I don't want to deal with some dipshit. Even if Holden convinced me this morning that I should, it's obvious that I'm in no shape to deal with the extra shit."

"I agree."

Which somehow makes me feel worse. I take a deep breath and take a step back from Nick. He rubs his jaw, but I suspect its frustration eating at him. "I think you should stay home and deal with what you are feeling."

"What?" Holden asks.

"If you're going to throw a tantrum instead of being willing to listen, you have no business being around someone we need to be professional with. So stay home." Nick walks away.

I just gape.

Since when does voicing concerns and asserting boundaries make me a child? Fuck that. I narrow my eyes and turn around, going to my room and fighting the urge to slam the door just so I don't validate him.

I try to lie down, but as soon as I hear the front door slam, I get up and pace the penthouse. I want to do something. Throw something, do anything to make me feel like I have control. But I call my mother.

"Hi, honey. Did you get a-"

"Show me the damn lists."

"Sophia!" She gasps. "You do not speak to me like-"

"I am not a child!" I almost yell. I pinch the bridge of my nose. "This is *my* wedding. I shouldn't be on someone else's schedule, Mom. I need copies of the list so I can cross things off as they're done or I'm going to lose my mind."

My mom is silent for a moment. "We need to do a spa day. That wasn't scheduled until-"

"I don't give a fuck when it was scheduled because I didn't schedule it."

"You should be on your way to a dinner right now." I hear her muffle the phone before saying something. "We are."

"I was uninvited. I'm sure you can imagine why. Send me the lists so I don't end up in another fight."

I hang up then rub my temples. Fuck this stress. Fuck all of this. We should have given ourselves more time. And now that's not even an option because invitations have already gone out.

I can't wait until this is over.

HOLDEN

"What happened in the few minutes I was gone?" I ask Nick in the town car.

"Sophie's too stressed for this." He's angry. He's in control, but barely. "She yelled at me, Holden. Over something that should have been a question. She didn't even let me answer."

"And then you called it a tantrum."

"Because I'm not in the wrong." His eyes cut to mine. "She threw a fit like a toddler. I will treat her like a toddler and put her in time out. I won't raise my voice. I won't yell at her, but I will not reward that kind of behavior."

He's talking about her like she's a child too. I arch an eyebrow and continue to watch him. As we pass block after block, I see him calm. He looks out the window, then closes his eyes and exhales. He'll reach the point I'm working to on his own, without me adding in.

"There's no right way to deal with this." He sighs.

"It's not easy, Nick. For any of us. And I agree she shouldn't have come, but there's a way to handle things that makes sure she knows her voice is heard while maintaining an actual conversation."

"I thought her mother had shared the plans with her. I didn't like being made the villain and didn't enjoy being yelled at," he says. "I didn't deserve it."

"I'm not saying you did."

"Why the fuck didn't we give ourselves more time?"

"The answer will not matter. We're in this position and Sophie is trying very hard to make sure the big things are taken care of. She doesn't care about napkins or paper for the menus or the DJ we selected, or the games. She doesn't care about a lot of the little things."

"I know." He scrubs over his face with his hand. "We should have gotten a real wedding planner, not just her mother. Who's idea was that?"

"Let's talk about all of this together, okay? With Sophie. Not about her." I suggest.

He nods and we arrive at the restaurant. Gunner opens the door, then his brow furrows. "Sophie?"

"She's having some alone time," I say for Nick. "She deserves a break."

"Carl is expecting her."

"Carl doesn't deserve time with our fiancée," Nick growls.

He's back to pissed. Gunner arches his eyebrow as Nick breezes past him and looks at me. "I missed something."

"It's a conversation for home, not here. Trust me," I whisper.

"Roman is going to ask."

"Not with Carl around."

And I'm proven right when we sit down. Carl's lips–thin as they are–turn up in a weasel-y smile that makes me want to deck him. Maybe all our tempers are heightened.

"And here I thought I was going to meet a one in a trillion woman."

Roman gives me a questioning look.

"Or perhaps she doesn't exist." Carl continues with a smugness I don't appreciate.

"My daughter exists," Miles says, scooting in with Diana at his side. "Wedding planning is hard work on top of a full-time job."

"Of course," Carl says with mock seriousness. "But who is this delightful creature?"

Diana freezes. She comes on to us all the time, but something about what Carl said bugs her. Miles takes her hand, showing off the giant diamond on her finger. "This is my lovely wife, Diana."

"I thought you were divorced." Carl's eyes narrow. "How out of the loop am I?"

"We gave it another go," Diana says. "It's excellent so far. So excellent we haven't had time to make proper announcements."

"Well, since I won't be meeting the amazing Sophia, perhaps we should talk business. Since you four are about to be married and will be hard pressed to start a family, how is this going to change things?"

Dear god. This is about to be a terrible dinner.

Carl digs into every facet and by the end, Roman has excused himself twice. When Carl orders dessert, Roman apologizes and says he needs to head out since he's not feeling well. Carl asks about the food and then demands to know if we took him to a place that's less than five stars.

Gunner rolls his eyes. "We're treating. Be happy for that alone."

"Perhaps I should sell a few of my stocks. I'm not sure how well you can expand a business if you all are distracted by domestic affairs.

That seems to be the case. At least at this dinner. A part of me wonders if this marriage is even real. Or is it just a clumsy attempt to drum up more business–the high-end kind since no formal announcements have gone out? I didn't even receive an invitation."

"We agreed that it would only be close friends and family. Nothing to do with work," I say.

Carl puts a hand to his chest. "I assumed we were friends."

"Acquaintances. We've never met your wife," Nick says.

"Don't have one. I prefer to live the fun life–meaning getting what I want and moving on. Something I thought Gunner and I both understood."

"I did until Sophie came along. She's better than having a different model on my arm every week." Gunner shrugs. "She's worth more than I deserve."

Carl is fucking up again and again. He seems to realize it after dinner. He offers to meet up at the end of the week instead if that works for our schedule. We agree to get back to him, then head home.

Diana stops me, rubs my biceps with a slight smile, then shakes her head. "What is wrong with Sophie? She yelled at me."

"Why didn't you share the plans with her like you did with us?"

"She didn't need to be more stressed," She pouts. "I was handling it."

"She thought it was forgotten, and it started a fight. She's not a child. This is her wedding, and she deserves to stay in the loop. Not knowing doesn't help any with her stress," I say.

Miles crosses his arms over his chest. "A fight?"

"Not now." I point at him.

When we get home, I see Roman sitting with Sophie. She's still all bristled, but Roman is using his soft voice, the one saved just for her.

"I'm sorry, Bambina. We thought she shared it with you after Nick talked to her."

"She didn't." There's the same tone. "And now I feel like some bitchy little girl being all unreasonable just because I want to know what's going on with my wedding."

"You're not. I'll take off Friday after lunch and we'll go to city hall and fill out everything we need to, okay? The marriage certificate will be approved and then everything will be legal. I'm sure the guys will join us too."

"We will," Gunner agrees.

Sophie looks up at us, then at Nick. She's still seething. Nick scratches the back of his head. "I'm sorry for my tone."

She keeps glaring. "I'm not ... happy."

"I understand," Nick says. "I'm not either."

"We're not going to sleep like this," I say. If it takes me saying something to get through all these thick heads, then I will. "We're about to be married, that means we have to learn to deal with this shit. We're airing everything out and then we're going to move on."

Sophie turns her glare on me. I shake my head at her. "Don't you give me that look. We're all adults. That means owning our mistakes, coming to an understanding, and forgiving each other when we have a problem. If we can't do that, we have no business in this relationship."

She takes a slow breath and rubs the back of her neck. "I felt like you didn't see me as an adult because I'm so much younger. That's why I lost my temper. I'm stressed too. It doesn't matter how much you guys are helping–I mean ... it does, because it shows how much you care–there's just so much for us to do and so little time and it's eating at me."

No one dares to cut her off now.

"I'm sorry, Nick. Next time I'm ... frustrated, I will make myself listen instead of assuming the worst." Sophie meets his eyes without glaring. "I'm still not super happy with my mother, but now I know the situation and I was wrong to yell at you."

"You yelled?" Roman asks.

She sinks between her shoulders. "Yes."

"I'm sorry for getting pissy." Nick clears his throat. "Your tone and accusation flipped a switch since I knew I did nothing wrong and I acted defensively. Rather than talking, I shut you down and put you in time out."

He takes a few steps toward her. "I'm sorry and I'll work to be better for you. By the time I was in the car, I was more pissed at myself than you. I think the wedding is getting to me, but I will work hard to put myself in your shoes before lashing out."

"Thank you," Sophie whispers.

Nick sits next to her and offers his hand. "Are we okay?"

She nods and takes his hand. "I'm sorry."

"It's okay."

They hug and I nod. One battle fought and gone through. I sit on the other couch with Gunner. Gunner shakes his head. "We're going crazy over the wedding and everything else."

"So let's look at all the lists we have, let's print them out, and let's cross off what we have done, designate some things, and make sure nothing's missing." I decide. "And let's try to avoid staying late at work."

"I can designate more work to those under me. I know that one of them is looking for a promotion and that means more responsibility." Nick offers.

Roman nods. "I've been in the process of hiring an assistant specific to me. Someone who can look over the legal stuff and help me balance my workload better. Not that you aren't excellent at scheduling for me, Sophia, I just need more help with the meetings I have."

"I know it's not personal." She assures him with a convincing smile.

"Gunner?" I ask.

He nods. "I'll see what I can do. Maybe if I work instead of finding ways to procrastinate, I'll be able to get home sooner."

Sophie wipes at her eyes. "We're too stressed. We need to find a way–other than sex–to get some things off our shoulders."

"Date night?" Gunner asks. "Something silly? Bowling or putt-putt?"

Sophie nods. "That would be nice. I miss group dates."

"This is not a great time," I say, preparing Sophie. "But I'd rather talk about it now. Carl still wants to meet you, Sophie. He asked if we could do Friday or Saturday."

"Saturday," she says. "Am I allowed to have an attitude with him?"

"You better." Gunner smirks. "Because I don't want to be alone in that respect."

I roll my eyes, but at least it's progress. We have an agreement; we survived the first fight before the wedding and I know there will be more. Sophie relaxes a little and I smile. "In better news, your mom mentioned you love your dress."

Sophie nods then blushes. "I don't know if my dad will, but it makes me feel like a princess. I'm excited for you guys to see it."

"If you don't tear up, I'm going to pinch you, Hold." Gunner hisses in my ear. "As a warning."

"And I'm excited about the menu." Roman smiles, for the first time in a while, he is at full power as he tells us all about it.

We all pitch in on what we've been working on and Sophie shows us the song that she's picked for her father-daughter dance.

This smiling, this fun, this is what makes us work and I'm going to fight tooth and nail to make sure everyone remembers it. We left war on the battlefield; we're not bringing it into a marriage.

SOPHIE

I wake up in my bed and hate it. After our long conversation last night, we agreed that I'd go to bed alone and finish destressing. Just like we also agreed we're not having sex for two weeks before the wedding–for tradition–so I have to get used to nights without at least one cuddle buddy.

I hate it. I thought it would just be a night before thing, but at least we have an earmark for a group night. I stretch and see an email from my mom, apologizing for trying to take the weight off my shoulder and admitting she did it the wrong way.

And a text from my dad asking about the fight and if I considered ending the engagement. I roll my eyes and tell him nothing, not even an apocalypse, could get me to call off the wedding.

Even when I was at my angriest, the thought of not going through with the wedding to *all* of them never crossed my mind. I love my guys, flaws and all. They don't reject me for my temper when it flairs. They don't judge me, don't put me down. We just have to figure out how to get through the prickly patches, and since we've had so few, it's all-new territory.

When I fought with my ex-boyfriend, it was just the two of us. We'd battle it out, fuck it out, then come to a conclusion. I don't want those battles with my guys. That's not the life I'm signing up for.

I start breakfast in the kitchen, wanting to set at least one tradition. I want to make sure we all have breakfast together whenever possible. It's the best way for all of us to start the day on the right foot. Roman kisses me before going for the food and I exchange I love yous with all my office working fiancés before they leave.

Nick even gives me an extra kiss and a hug before he leaves. Holden is last. I pull out something special for him, a little mini apple pie because I know he loves them. He looks from it to me and leans his head to the side.

"You handled last night better than anyone, Holden. Don't think that I didn't realize how much easier you made everything." I hand him the pie. "I wanted to thank you with something other than words."

He sets it to the side and takes both my hands, holding them against his chest. "I love you, Sophie. I love my friends too and I don't like fighting in the house. I know we have to figure things out still, but I don't need thanks for pulling my weight in this relationship."

I hug him. "You don't even realize how much of a catch you are. You are pure gold magic, Hold."

He chuckles and holds me. Something shifts and he squeezes me tighter. "Do you know how much I'd do to keep you from being upset? How much I'd give up to make sure that you are here every morning?"

"I didn't even think about leaving."

"From what I've heard, the fights get worse the closer we get to the wedding. I'm pretty sure that engagement is a way for people to see the worst in each other."

"Well, we've all seen I can be extra bitchy when I'm jumping to conclusions. But I know you guys wouldn't cheat on me and I think that's the only thing that would make me walk away," I say. "Not encouraging anyone to be a dick, just … just saying."

"And none of us are capable of that."

Holden and I get through the day working and throwing snacks for the other person to catch in their mouth. We keep track of the points and I'm better, but that might mean Holden has a better aim.

He nails me in the forehead with a skittle and I rub the spot. He laughs and shakes his head. "You have a green stain now."

"Hold!"

"Yes, ma'am." Gunner picks me up, leaving me breathless. He looks at my forehead and shakes his head. "Green isn't your color, Sweets."

He licks the spot, making me squeal as I shove at him.

We end up playing a new board game that night, then Nick and I play chess as Gunner makes dinner–only wearing an apron and boxers. Roman rolls his eyes as he takes care of something wedding related.

I play a song, then shake my head and change it before making my move on the chess board. Nick rubs his chin. "I can't tell what you're doing."

"That makes two of us," I tease.

He chuckles and in another four moves, he has me beat.

I don't mind though. I've found one of my first dance songs. I play it again and see Gunner perk up. "I love this song."

"Yeah?" I ask.

"John Legend is amazing. I love it. I'm claiming it." He points at everyone with a spatula. "Mine."

Nick rolls his eyes. "I have a song for you to listen to … for us."

My heart beats in my chest. How could I have yelled at him when he's so good to me? I never should have crossed that line.

"My mom said we should look into dance lessons," I say. All the guys laugh and I look at them. "What?"

"We all know how to dance, Soph," Gunner says.

"Really?"

Another slow song plays and Nick offers me his hand. I take it and he sweeps me into a dance. My feet follow his obediently. I don't feel like I'm dancing at all. I'm floating. He twirls me under his arm, and Holden steps in.

I giggle as he dips me and kisses me, then spins me under both his arms so my back is against his front. "Salsa and tango."

When he spins me out, I fall into Gunner. He chuckles and I brace myself for club dancing. "I can waltz too. Mom insisted I learn to impress girls in high school."

And he shows me what he means, twirling me and sweeping me all across the room, before he bows and puts my hand on Roman's. Roman claims my eyes and dances with me in a way that makes me swoon all over again.

He keeps me close enough that no one can cut in, but far enough that it's like a tease. I want to be crushed against him, feeling every one of his heartbeats thrum through my body. When the song ends, he spins me out, so I end up by myself.

"Wow." I put my hand to my chest. "How is there so much I still don't know about you guys?"

"That's what keeps life interesting." Gunner swats my bottom.

I laugh and we spend the next two days having a good time as we go over the wedding until I get a call from the florist in Paris. They speak perfect English, but that doesn't make me like them any more. Apparently, they ended up double booked and can't help on the wedding day.

I want to hit something, throw something, but take ten deep breaths, like Nick and I promised to do when our tempers get triggered. Not that it matters, because five minutes later, I'm with Roman and the guys on the way to city hall to apply for the marriage license.

My foot taps and Gunner's the one that asks. "Sweets ... what's eating at you?"

"The florist canceled." I hiss.

"There are plenty in Paris." Nick shrugs. "That's not as terrible as it seems and at least we know now."

"You're not annoyed?"

"Very," Holden huffs. "They never should have double booked, but we have to fix it, not focus on what should have been."

Nick nods.

"But I'm not wrong to be annoyed?"

"It's an inconvenience." Gunner pats my knee. "But it's not like something's wrong with your dress."

"When are you guys getting your tuxes?"

Roman soothes me this time, stroking the back of my neck and kneading the muscles that are tight there. "Tomorrow, before dinner with Carl."

"While you're at the spa," Nick says. "Full body massage, pampering, skin treatments, anything and everything you want."

I nod. Luckily, the marriage certificate is easy to get set up, and then we're off to putt-putt where I destroy all my men. I think Gunner's too busy taking pictures of all of us and pointing at all the terrifying animals–their faces are half rubbed off thanks to age–and I see Roman's hackles raise.

He hits the ball on the last hole and it ends up in the pond. A string of curses in Italian leave his lips, but I rub his chest and kiss his throat. "You're just too strong for this game, amore. It's sexy as hell."

"It's a ball in a hole," he growls.

"It's okay, Roman. It's not like it's a reflection of how you handle putting things in other holes," Gunner teases.

The mom-kid combo behind us gasps. She claps her hands over her son's ears and gives Gunner a hate-filled look. He shrugs. "He'll learn about it soon enough, ma'am."

I tug Gunner's shirt and shake my head. "Don't take the fun out of his learning."

Nick gets a hole in two and Holden ends up circling the hole until he nudges it in with his foot. He reaches in, then looks at me in confusion. "It's a pipe?"

"It keeps you from going around again for free," I say with a shrug.

Roman is still all coiled and frustrated, but I know how to fix that.

"You know the important holes," I whisper in his ear as we head back to the car. "The ones that make me happy."

"I'm better at soccer." He huffs.

"Bring it, all-star." Gunner demands. "One on one."

Roman rolls his eyes. "Soph would be upset if you were bruised for the wedding."

"Yes, I would!" I agree, but can't stop the laugh. "Play nice."

"Make me." Gunner puts his hands up, like he's ready to fight Roman right here and now. "I can take him."

"Well, you could fight Roman." I offer, making Gunner smile. "Or we can all go home and you can *all* play with me."

All four of my sexy men look me over at that comment. I smile and let myself into the town car. "It's up to you. The longer we take here, the less time we have before the exhaustion kicks in and knocks me out."

Nick is the first one in and steals my mouth in a kiss that threatens to set me on fire. That seems to decide it. I'm passed around as we drive, kissed, stroked, teased with soft touches and dirty promises whispered in my ear.

I'm convinced the only reason we make it home without me being defiled right there in the car is because there's no partition and as much as my men like sharing me, they don't want anyone else to see.

In the elevator, they take it up a notch, half stripping me as I grind between them and accept kisses across my neck, my mouth, my shoulder, until the elevator dings. I get out first and walk backward against our front door as I smile at my guys.

"Still love me after I kicked all your asses in putt-putt?"

"I think it's fair," Roman murmurs as he eyes me.

My dress is bunched around my hips and one strap is half way down my arm. I lick my puffy bottom lip and lean back against the door, pushing my chest out and fighting the urge to stroke myself just to show them what they could be doing.

"Oh yeah?" I ask.

"Considering that means we get to reward you." His naughty smile makes my knees shake. Roman tangles his fingers in my hair and jerks back to claim me in a kiss that leaves nothing to the imagination.

Tonight will fix everything based on this little preview alone.

NICK

We take advantage of everything Sophie offers and damn, what a package she is. Her face flushes as Holden and I finger her together and she sucks Gunner's cock. Roman licks and sucks her nipples while holding one thigh wide in his big hand.

She moans and pants despite the slick sounds of Gunner moving in and out of her throat. It doesn't take her long to come apart and Gunner groans as she ups the pace, her eyes wild, hair bunched in his hands.

Holden moves to get something, and I take that opportunity to thrust right into Sophie's dripping pussy. She groans and her eyes flick to me as she nods. Good. I need her hard and fast, need her to know how intensely I love her.

"You're amazing, Sophie," I groan, grinding my hips against hers to get even deeper inside her.

Her mouth pops free of Gunner's cock and she turns to take Holden's in her mouth while Rubbing Gunner's in her right hand. He moans and continues to guide her head. "Take Hold hard and deep, just like he deserves, Sweets. Show him everything that sassy mouth can do."

"Ready, Bambina?" Roman asks.

She groans and nods, her body rolling against mine as I rub her clit and thrust into her again. She takes Holden so deep she gags..

Sophie pants and I see her hand tighten on Gunner. Her moans keep me hard and determined to satisfy. Groaning around Holden's cock, her body tenses, then relaxes around me.

Roman grins. "Such a good girl. You take us so well."

Her eyes haze over before she shuts them. Roman swats her ass as I thrust into her as deeply as I can. I grip her legs, tightening my hold so I can make sure I hit the spot that drives her insane.

Roman rubs her clit and goes to her tits, kissing, biting, and sucking as I fuck her hard. Jesus, she steals my breath away. Naked, covered with marks, sucking Holden off as her face goes red. She's just as beautiful as she is when she's all put together.

I should have known I'd never be able to resist her. From the moment I saw her, I knew we belonged like this. I can tell she's close by the way her body writhes under mine, and I know it's going to be a struggle to wait until she comes to finish.

"Fuck, Soph. Come. Don't hold out on me," I growl.

She jerks Holden forward, choking herself on him as she comes apart for us. Holden's body trembles as he finishes, and I follow close behind. Gunner switches spots with me and flips Sophie so she's on her knees.

"Mm. You taste good, Hold," she pants.

He kisses her as Gunner rocks into her. He spreads her legs wide and groans. "Fuck, you have such a sexy little ass, Sophie."

She groans as he fucks her hard, then almost slow motion so he can watch every inch disappear in and out of her. Holden releases her and lets Roman take over. I watch them share her, watch how she bounces between them, legs shaking, body slick with sweat as she tries to focus on their pleasure as much as her own.

But I can't resist touching. I slip a hand under her to squeeze and massage one of her breasts. Holden swats her ass, making it bloom red before biting the back of her shoulder, something we all know she loves.

And she deserves to be fucked as thoroughly as possible. Roman purrs to her in Italian as he knots his fingers in her hair and guides her mouth over his cock. She comes two more times before Roman and Gunner finish.

We linger in the living room then. I don't know about the others, but I'm too exhausted to move. It's been a fucking long day and as much as I enjoy spending time with Sophie, I can feel myself power down and I know I need a break.

Sophie gets up and I catch her in my lap as she stumbles while stepping over Gunner. She chuckles and kisses me. "Shower?"

I nod and get up, using one hand to support my back. She rubs my hip as we get to the bathroom. "Are you okay?"

"Just pulled a muscle," I say.

She nods and washes me first, then I tickle her sides until she squeals and takes over, soaping over her lovely curves until I can pull her close and kiss her temple. "You know I love you, right?"

"I know."

"The fight doesn't change that."

"If it did, we'd be in trouble," she teases, then kisses my chest. "I love you too, Nick. You're a good man and I'm sorry again for being so high-strung."

"Does that mean I get a peek at the dress?"

"Hell no." She swats my ass. "That's bad luck. Since I'm marrying all four of you in front of a crowd, we'll need all the luck we can get."

We're both quiet for a moment, just enjoying the hot water. Then she swallows. "Did Matthew and Bella reply yet?"

"I don't know. We'll have to check the website. We can do that once we're all cleaned up."

"Does that mean you're pulling out the projector again?" She bounces a little. "Do you know how sexy it is that you're technically savvy like that?"

I whisper meaningless technical computer terms in her ear and feel her rub against me. If we don't stop now, I know that we're going to end up going another round and that will knock me out.

I kiss the top of her head. "Easy, sweetheart. We still have a full day tomorrow too, so I can't sleep in."

"I'm very okay with whatever happens at the wedding." She sighs, turning off the water.

I arch an eyebrow and she gives me a naughty smile. "As soon as it's over, the honeymoon starts, which means sex and fun can be the main priority."

Grinning, I haul her out of the shower, wrap her up in a towel and pull on a robe of my own. We head back to the living room, where I set up the projector. We look over the RSVP list. Of course, Valerie and her parents have already confirmed, along with Roman's mother, Massimo, Hunter, and Chase, then Matthew.

Not too bad. Gunner points out his parents and Holden just kind of sits there until he sees his brother's name pop up. He shoots me a glare. "I told you not to invite anyone."

"Your brother heard about it from General Marcos. He called me." I defend myself.

"And you didn't tell me?"

"I wanted to make it a surprise. I knew that if I told you before the invitation went out, you'd be angry." I shrug. "He wants to support you, Holden. Aaron isn't that bad."

Sophie sits in his lap and kisses his neck. I'm sure she's whispering sweet things in his ear, but I shrug and continue scrolling through. We have eleven people confirmed so far.

"And I'll take care of the florists tomorrow," Gunner says. "Shouldn't be hard."

"High school French going to get you through all that?" Roman teases.

"I speak it fluently. I told you, I'm great at procrastinating." He snorts. When I arch an eyebrow at him, he shrugs. "If I get stuck, there's always that translation app that works in real time."

And that seems to take care of everything.

We head to bed, meaning Sophie is with me since I know we're still a little raw after our fight. I cling to her in the morning, then kiss her temple as I get up. I promise we'll see her later, but she just snorts out something nonsensical before rolling into the spot I left.

She clutches my pillow close, inhales, and snuggles in. How can she be so sweet and so fiery at the same time? I shake my head, forcing myself to get ready for the fitting, or I know I just won't go.

Sophie's that tempting.

But I get up with the guys, head to the luxurious shop, and try on a few different tuxes. Gunner looks at his pink tie, straightens it, and nods, but I can tell something's bugging him. Roman sighs. "Out with it."

"What if we all did white ties to match Sophie's dress and did colored button-ups instead? I think it would look better."

The men working go to work, pulling out the matching button-ups for each tie. We change, do the white ties and Gunner still looks dissatisfied. I don't blame him. The white feels out of place.

"May I make a suggestion?" Giorgio, the shop owner, says.

"Always," Roman responds.

Apparently, they go way back. A family thing, I'm sure. Giorgio pulls Gunner in front, then takes off his jacket. He looks at the color of his shirt, the original color of the tie, then suggests doing a lining in that color, so we can roll our sleeves and it will show. Then, with the traditional white button-up and colored tie, there will be more impact. It won't be as boring as Gunner feels, but we will still have all the clean crispness of the traditional look.

"Absolutely," Gunner says with a nod. "That's perfect. And it's not too much to do before we leave in two weeks?"

Giorgio shakes his head and reaches up to pat Roman's shoulder. "Anything for family."

With everything else approved, we head out. Gunner pauses outside the shop and faces Roman. "Okay, I know I've asked before."

"Not this again." I rub my forehead. It hasn't come up in over a year, and now that we've met Roman's family, it should be more obvious than ever, but Gunner's stuck and I know it. Holden nudges me and I sigh. "Fine, you win."

"I told you he wouldn't drop it after our trip." Holden beams, knowing he's not paying for a single drink tonight.

"Is your family in some old-time Italian mafia?" Gunner persists.

Roman rolls his eyes. "We've discussed this."

"Because a tuxedo shop is a great cover. That's all I'm saying. And Giorgio is a mafia name."

"Anything is a mafia name if it sounds Italian," Roman huffs. "Thank the movies for that."

We all laugh as we get back in the town car. I added getting Sophie's wedding band today since I was sure that we'd have the time.

Holden checks his phone and nods. "Sophie went for the deluxe package when she realized her mom was coming."

"As if her mom isn't going to add stress," Roman grumbles, frustrated. "We need to make sure she's cut off before she flirts on the wedding day."

"And take away so much fun?" Gunner puts a hand to his chest.

We get to the ring shop and I give Sophie's ring size so we can choose a band. We didn't all get her the same metal for her engagement rings, so I'm not sure what to go with. Gunner rubs his jaw.

"We could do white gold. It would work best with the combination."

"Since when did you become a stylist?" I ask.

He blushes. "I've been planning things with Val in order to make amends."

I can't stop the smile from spreading over my face. There's nothing any of us wouldn't do for Sophie.

SOPHIE

Once I step out of the spa, even with my mom on my arm, I feel better. Between the massages, the amazing aromatherapy, the music, and the constant pampering, I feel amazing. I'll just pretend the champagne has nothing to do with it.

Mom drags me to a small brunch place next. "Right before you leave, we'll go to the salon so you can get your hair refreshed, cut if you want, get your nails done, and get *everything* waxed."

"You are way too eager for that," I grumble.

She laughs and rubs my hand. "I know that the wedding is just a day. The closer you get, the simpler it will feel. Then you'll be thinking about all the things you will have wished you did to prepare for the honeymoon."

"*We* are not going lingerie shopping," I say. "That's me and Valerie."

She pouts, then laughs at my expression. "Of course. There are some things a mother doesn't need to know. However, I do need to know how all this is working."

"All what?" I ask.

"Well, beyond having sex with four men sharing you," she says, then trails off when the waiter's eyes bulge. She orders as if it's nothing and I do the same, but trip over my words twice. She continues when he leaves. "How is the planning going? Are they helping? Are they causing problems?"

"Only the one fight so far," I say while taking a drink from my water. "But we're meeting Carl tonight."

"Eew," she says. "He's a horrible little man. Putting others down to make up for his size."

"He's short?"

"No. He's little. Different thing." She shows me her fingers only an inch apart and I get the picture. "Overcompensating is common in business, but he thinks he's a ladies' man. Not like your men. I bet they don't have a thing to compensate for."

"Mom!" I hiss.

"I'm curious, is all. This is all new to me." She leans forward, waiting for me to launch into an erotica-level story about how well-hung my fiancés are.

I feel my face go hot and stir my straw in my drink. "It's new to me, too. I love them all. I want to be with them forever, but it's not like we've made a big show of being together as a group. I'm sure Roman's family noticed when we were in Italy, but it's been an unspoken thing and now that everyone is going to know, I just kind of feel … I feel like they're going to judge."

"If they do, it's their issue, not yours." Mom takes my hand. "I mean it, Sophie. And you have bigger balls than I did."

"What do you mean?"

She sighs. "I encouraged your father to elope this time around. I didn't want to deal with our family and friends scoffing at it after our very public and nasty divorce. I was sure they'd make comments about how if we didn't work out once, we would not work out again."

"Mom." I hold her hand tighter. "No one would-"

"Oh yes, they would. It didn't stop some of my old college friends from reaching out once I changed my status on Facebook. Catty bitches." She shakes her head. "The point is the people that talk shit are ones that don't deserve your time and don't need to be in your life. Which means they shouldn't be able to afford the cost of the flight."

I laugh, and we clink our glasses together before digging into lunch. We talk about the wedding, Mom tries again to get me to draw her a picture of how a five-way works, then she drops me off at home feeling better than I have in weeks.

Last night, I got a fantastic date night and had amazing sex. Today I got pampered until I felt like a princess. Plus, things feel better with my mom. I'm on the verge of climbing up to cloud nine and claiming it as my own when I remember dinner tonight.

It's so tempting to say fuck it and cancel again because Carl sounds like a major dick, but I can't do that to my guys. They've done plenty for me and it's time for me to even that out. Plus, I know he's important in terms of business and took me not showing up as some kind of slight.

When the guys get home, they find me trying to choose between dresses. Nick steps up and hands me the navy one. It's a nice tea-length dress with a sweetheart neckline and sleeves that hang off my shoulders.

I press my lips to his cheek and wiggle out of my comfy clothes to pull it on.

"Hold up. I want to enjoy the view for a second," Gunner says, lying on my bed on his belly with his feet up as he looks me over. "Delicious."

I roll my eyes but smile anyway. "No way I can tempt you all into having the stomach flu and having fun with me at home instead of dealing with this dick?"

"Nope," Roman says from behind me, pressing his face to my hair before dropping a kiss on the back of my neck. It feels more intimate than anything he's done so far for some reason, and the shiver that teases my spine proves it. "We're going," he purrs.

"What if I start a fight?"

"Going," Holden says, putting my other dress back.

"Cramps?" I try again.

Nick smiles, shakes his head and says. "Going."

"I'm feeling very outnumbered right now." I huff.

Roman chuckles and whispers Italian in my ear. "Let me show you off."

Damn, there's no winning with that tone of voice. So we end up in a limo and pick Carl up on the way. I dislike him immediately. He flashes fancy clothes, an expensive watch, and his tom-cat eyes don't leave my tits when he introduces himself.

I look at Roman and arch an eyebrow. I'd appreciate a nice display of male dominance or ownership here. It's Gunner that speaks up and puts a possessive hand on my thigh. "As you can see, Sophie is very real."

"Absolutely." He licks across his bottom lip, then meets my eyes. "To think you're Miles's daughter."

"I am," I say.

Roman pulls out his phone, then hands it to me. Carl smirks. "And such an excellent secretary that you earned wife status."

I freeze, take a slow breath, and Roman rubs the back of my neck. "It's wedding-related. Sophie doesn't work for us. She's a colleague."

"Really? She's not the receptionist? I know she could drum up a lot of business if she was made more … available."

Please let his condo or hotel room catch on fire so we can avoid this. I keep praying for that before I remember to read Roman's phone. Massimo wanted to remind us he's bringing Danny and the baby as well.

I nod to Roman. "I like Danny. She's fun."

"Very," he agrees. "I think she and your mother will get along well."

I like the thought of that. Then my guys will be *mine*. No sharing and no Mom asking cringey questions she finds hilarious. Not that it stops Carl from asking things along the same subject line. It sounds so much skeevier coming from him because he expects an answer.

"Enough," Holden warns. "We're going to be professional."

"Professional among friends is no fun." Carl chuckles.

Thankfully, we get to the restaurant and I fling myself out of the limo first. Nick comes up behind me, takes my hand, and kisses my cheek. "We started a timer."

"How long?"

"An hour." I see my frustration reflected in his face.

"I will not make it that long without saying something," I say. "I don't think I have the patience to be nice."

Nick turns me around to where Roman is towering over Carl, his face so terrifying that I almost don't recognize him. I can't hear what he says, but the color drains from Carl's face and he holds his hands up before rushing inside before any of us.

Gunner slings his arm around my waist and narrows his eyes at Nick. "I'm telling you. Mafia."

I shake my head at him but thank Roman before we head inside. Roman sits next to Carl, leaving Nick and Gunner to sit next to me. Holden watches from his place at the head of the table. I swear he's the ref between Carl and the others.

"So, Sophie, how did you get involved in the business?" he asks, a slight tremor to his voice.

I lean forward and wrap my lips around the straw of my drink, very aware of how intently he's watching me. He bothered the hell out of me the entire ride in the limo, it's my turn to twist things.

I swallow and rub my arm, which pushes my breasts together to create even more cleavage. "Well, I worked hard in college, then grad school. Dad's been in business longer than I can remember and it let him travel, see the world, be his own boss and it sounded like my kind of work."

He nods, pats his temple with the napkin, and struggles to keep his eyes on my face until I shrug and his gaze drops. I smirk. "Plus, it means I'm in New York and brought me to the four best men the world's ever created."

Gunner strokes up the inside of my thigh and I take an unsteady breath. His chest brushes my arm as he whispers in my ear. "Stop baiting him or Roman is going to toss him out with the trash."

I give him my most innocent face and Gunner digs his nails into my thighs despite the smile teasing the corner of his lips. I shrug, then sweep my hair over my shoulder, showing off the two bite marks and a single hickey that I didn't bother to cover with makeup.

"How did you get involved with my fiancés?" I ask Carl.

He goes into some winding circular story that is hands down the most boring and confusing thing I've ever heard. I look over to Nick for translation. "He was a stockbroker, saw the rise, and got involved before we opened the second location."

"Ah."

"Well, if you want to simplify it." Carl takes a long drink from his glass.

We get through dinner and I take a page from my mom's book. If Carl's allowed to ask invasive personal questions I do the same, pretending to be drunk. I like the flustered look on his face, the hungry, pleased glint to Roman's eyes whenever he catches my gaze, and the way Gunner and Nick tease me with feather-light touches.

Holden takes it all in, only speaking when someone addresses him. Which I hope doesn't mean I'm bothering him. By the time Carl looks at the time and makes an excuse about an early flight, I pout.

"We were just getting to the good part. Don't you want to come out and dance with us? Gunner has some new moves he wants to try out and we could use a friend." I pout.

Carl gulps. "I'm not a friend. I'm more of an acquaintance. I'll see myself out."

He runs for the hills and I smirk. "I don't think he'll be a problem anymore."

"You're impossible, Sophie," Holden murmurs, but then I see him smile. "But what a wedding present–getting Carl out of our hair."

"To Sophie!" The guys toast me and I fan myself.

Maybe this wedding stuff is overblown. I can relax and let it all be taken care of by my mom and just give the final say on things without worrying. Especially with the promise of forever hanging in front of me.

ROMAN

The next week is murdering me. Sophia started out easygoing, seeming to enjoy where we were in the planning, able to relax. Her normal self returned to us until she got a call saying there were changes to the dress–that the seamstress had misunderstood something or other.

Then it was rage. Of course, after that, our number one DJ backed out, the venue wanted to up the charge, and they all called Sophia. Sophia, who's trying to work and hold on to her sanity without letting it slip away.

By Thursday, she's an unpacked mess of stress living in oversized t-shirts and nothing else. Holden nominates me to handle it this time while he and Gunner check on the tuxes and take care of the DJ issue. Nick is sorting out the Hotel and making sure we have the wedding bands on time.

So I have to get Sophia back to a happy place and get her packing. We're going to be leaving for Paris in two days and I don't have the patience to wait until we're in the air to calm her down.

When I get home, I see her on the phone, face red, eyes furious. She yells and hangs up before gripping her messy hair. Without missing a beat, I toss her over my shoulder and head to my bathroom.

"Put me down!" She squeals. "I'm not in the mood!"

"We're showering," I say instead.

"Don't you bark orders at me!"

I swat her ass. She keeps struggling on my shoulder, but I turn on the shower–a cold one–and put her under the water. She squeaks and I let her slide down my body. She glowers at me despite the fact that she's soaking wet.

"What the fuck, Roman?" She hisses.

"You looked heated, and not in the way I like."

"That doesn't mean you can go and be a caveman!"

Oh, but it does. I'm just as frustrated as she is. I'm over all the issues. I'm over the shit coming up at work. I'm over Miles giving me a deadline to come back because I'm second in command. I'm over everything that's keeping my life from being easy.

So I take off my shirt and toss it to the side, then start on my pants.

Sophia takes a step back. "What are you–"

"I'm pissed."

"At me?" She shivers.

I sigh and change the heat of the water. I can't manage the flesh-burning heat she likes, but I can meet in the middle. I shuck my pants and boxers off, then close the distance between us.

Sophie squirms, her eyes all big. "At me?"

"No." I tip her chin up. "Not at you."

"So why–"

I kiss her hard and deep. God, I haven't touched her in so long. I devour her tongue as she opens for me, rubbing my sides and accepting me without question. Holden may talk with her and be reasonable, Nick may argue, and Gunner … well I don't think he and Sophia have fought at all, but I know the words can come better when we're calm.

A lesson I learned in Hawaii, but I don't want us to get to that point again.

I kiss across her throat and she groans, rubbing herself against me. "Roman."

"Bambina," I purr in her ear. "Why are you so furious?"

"So much is going wrong and I'm falling behind in work and haven't been sleeping. I don't feel like we're ready to get on a plane when there's so much still to do here," she whispers.

I press my forehead to hers and cup her face between my hands. "If I fuck you, will you sleep better?"

Her mouth opens, but no words come out. I take it as an invitation. I tug at her shirt, pulling it over her head so she doesn't have to try to breathe through the wet fabric, then tangle my hand in her wet hair as I lick deep into her mouth. This is all she gets until I get an answer.

"Yes, amore," she says. "It will help."

So I lift her thigh over my hip and rub my already hard cock against her pussy. She moans and grinds, creating more friction between us. I kiss her rougher, wrap my hand around her throat and cup her breast in my hand, teasing her nipple until she whimpers and squirms against me.

"Please!" She begs when I release her mouth, her lips all raw and puffy. "Please, Roman."

She doesn't complain about a single bite or spank. Moans when I push fingers into her and begs me for more even after she's come twice. I thrust into her and her back arches her head resting against the tile wall behind her. We fuck hard and fast, changing positions whenever I decide.

On the verge of her third orgasm, I join her, jerking out just in time to come across her ass. She pants and we slide to the floor together. Sophie snuggles in close and lets me rub her back as we catch our breath.

"I like that method," she murmurs against my throat.

"I knew you would." I swat the outside of her thigh. "Wild little thing."

She rubs over my chest and abdomen. "It's so easy to lose sight of the point of this with so much going on. I just want to be married to all four of you. I want us to have everything we planned. I want the vows, the cake, the dances, the happily ever after. But right now, I keep thinking how much easier it was to tell my dad about us than plan a single day. "

I kiss the top of her head. "I promise my vows will make you happy cry–if that helps."

"It does." She relaxes a little more against me. "And I know it will be worth it. I know that Roman, it's just … I feel like it's taking over our lives. I'm not being who I want to be, all of us are pulled in different directions to fix things. I know Dad keeps trying to chain you to the office."

I brush my fingers over her hip, then pick us both up, determined to clean up and get out of the shower before I say something I shouldn't. About how close I am to giving my notice, how badly I want to go on adventures with her and the guys. There's so much we didn't get to do in Italy, so much I want to show her when it comes to the world, and I can see the time slipping away from us in the daily routine.

"What?" She pulls my head down to look into my eyes. "You let me vent. Let's go. I can handle it. Even if it's you telling me what a bitch I am."

"I'd never say that, Bambina," I say. "Never."

"Then tell me what's going on in that head. You're full of mysteries that I want to know."

I sigh. "You're right. Miles wants me in the office a couple weeks after we get married. I've been arguing with him about it. I don't want to work my whole life away and then look back and see all the missed time. I feel like I'm half-assing my time with you."

"You do?" Her face scrunches up in confusion. "I never feel that way."

"When I'm with you, I'm always counting down until I have to be back at work which makes me feel twice as pressured to pack the most into every moment. When I'm at work, all I'm doing is thinking about how I'd rather be home with you, or traveling, or checking things off my bucket list."

She rubs my chest, spreading the suds across my body as I organize my thoughts. "Gunner has always encouraged me to go out and have fun. He's always asked what the point of all this money is if we don't put it to use and I thought I was the smart one but now..."

"Now you think he knows a thing or two?" She smiles. "He's eccentric, but he's not stupid." She pushes me under the water to rinse me off. "And neither are you, Roman. It's your life. Even when we're married, I want you to be happy, to feel fulfilled."

"I want children, Bambina. We didn't talk about it, but ... I do."

"It's been on my mind too. It's not a no, but... I want to enjoy what we have more first. I would love to have a sweet baby Roman running around the house. But once we have kids, a lot has to be adjusted and we won't have alone time like this. We won't be able to travel for years and even then, it will be different."

I swallow hard and work on soaping her up as she tells me all the places she wants to go, all the things she wants to try. When I rub soap down her spine, my hand stops. She looks over her shoulder and I hesitate again.

"Do not tell the guys this."

"Secrets, Roman-"

"I've been thinking about retiring." I'm not sure that she hears me over the shower, but she turns and looks up at me with wide eyes. I nod. "I've been thinking about it for a while now. Since before I proposed and … and I don't know. It hasn't gone away."

"If that's what you want, you know I'll support you." She hugs me. "I want you to be happy, Roman. I'm biased because I want you to be happy while married to me, but that's it. If you want to retire, if you want to try something new, do it. You only get one life."

I shake a little as I cling to her. This whole shower and sex thing was supposed to be about calming her down, but considering how she's speaking to me in Italian, telling me how much she appreciates me, how good I am, and calling me a puppy, I feel like it's done more for me.

"I'm not ready to tell the guys, not until I know what I'm doing. It's … a big choice."

"I think we can survive on four salaries rather than five." She laughs, standing on her toes and kissing my chin. "Now rinse me off and let's go cuddle."

I chuckle but obey, dragging a clean shirt over her body once she's dried off and pulling on boxers so we can cuddle while watching a movie. Sophia plays with my hair and hums along with the TV before she pauses. I catch her looking at her engagement rings with a soft, warm smile.

"Help me pack tonight?"

"Am I allowed to?"

"Everything you're not allowed to see isn't in the house. You think I trust any of you to not look for things you shouldn't?" She arches a brow. "The best secret is one that's not tempting."

"It's all with Valerie?"

She frowns. "That obvious?"

"Don't tell Gunner," I advise. "He's meeting with her and going over wedding plans."

Sophia gapes. "What?"

"Oh yes. It's very hush-hush. All secretive," I tease, kissing the worry line on her forehead. "He's trying to get on better terms with her for you. He doesn't want her to not feel welcome or you to feel like you have to choose."

Her eyes water and she hides her face against my neck. "I will never do enough to deserve you guys."

I pull her onto my lap and hug her before pressing my lips to her ears. "How do you think we feel, Sophia? Why do you think Nick is bargaining and fixing two things today? Why do you think Gunner learned French? Or why Holden's coming out of his shell to keep the peace?"

"I'm driving you all crazy with my anger?" she whimpers.

I laugh and shake my head. "We love you more than anything and we'll show it, through the big stuff right now and the little stuff later. You'll never forget, Bambina."

SOPHIA

I lie in bed trying to double-check that I have everything packed in my bags that I could need. I have so many kinds of clothes in there, for every kind of weather that could come up. I have plenty of lingerie and plenty of shoes. I even packed my favorite pillow and a sweatshirt that I stole from Holden.

I have a bunch of jewelry on top of what I have planned for my wedding day. I even have the bands for the guys. I've got some vows written too. All good things. I think talking with Roman and knowing that he's stuck in a few ways, unsure, and needing advice helped more than anything.

He's always been so put together. He rarely shows any kind of hesitation, any kind of self-doubt, that I just assumed he never had it. Our conversation in Hawaii was one thing, but him telling me he felt overwhelmed, that he felt like life was passing him by, and he wasn't as sure about his career or future as I'd assumed he was, made me feel more validated. More like an adult.

I roll in bed, then glare at the empty spot in my bed. Roman and I broke a rule. We had sex within the two weeks' window before the wedding, but I can't make myself care about that.

Not when I hate sleeping alone.

It's so much harder to feel secure and so much harder to fall asleep when I'm all alone. They've spoiled me with their attention, with the fact that they're more often against me, with me, touching me than not.

Groaning, I open my phone and text Holden.

Sophie: You up?

Holden: Is this a booty call?

I laugh and get up, walking to his office. He's stretched out on the couch reading. I've learned he only goes to his room to sleep or for sex. Everything else goes on outside of it. He says it makes for better sleeping, but I disagree considering my own issues.

Holden sets his book to the side–something about international economics, then opens his arms to me. I settle against him and hum.

"Not a booty call," I murmur.

"Good, because that's against the rules." He still presses his face to my hair and rubs my back. "All packed and ready?"

"More ready to marry you." I lift my face and his lips mold to mine.

I kiss him slow and soft, my tongue teasing him with gentle strokes until he groans and tightens his hand in my hair. "You're going to get me all worked up."

"I can't sleep," I explain, rubbing his chest through his thin shirt. "I don't like being in bed alone."

"Just another week." He promises. "Then no one will ask you to sleep by yourself."

"Unless you're mad at me." I huff.

He chuckles and kisses my temple. "I don't think there's ever been a time where all four of us are mad at you in one day, let alone at the same time."

"Yet," I grumble.

Holden keeps playing with my hair and rubbing my back. "Anything you're worried about?"

"Not right now. Roman's picking up the marriage certificate tomorrow before we leave. We have almost everyone RSVP'd. Venues are set, the dress is fixed, and everything is checked off the list."

"You got the song for our dance?" Holden asks. "I'm curious."

"Come Away With Me by Nora Jones," I answer, then scroll through my phone to select it on Spotify.

Holden smiles down at me and kisses my forehead. "It's perfect."

"Good, because I love cuddling you and how safe you make me feel. All the adventures we go on, the way you're soft and tender with me, just like the music." I squeeze him. "I love you so much."

"I love you, Sophie." He promises, kissing me. "Everything is going to go fine at the wedding."

"Are you sure?"

"Not even a little." He laughs. "But that's the nice thing about it. Only the people planning it know how it's supposed to turn out. We have the idea in our heads, but no one else knows what to expect, so they'll be blown away no matter what."

"It's official." I beam at him. "Whenever I'm overwhelmed, I'm coming to you. You're the best at talking sense into me."

He kisses my forehead. "And you're the only woman that's made me confident enough to share what I know."

"You know so much." I rub down his hip. "I'm pissed at anyone who makes you feel you should hide."

Holden keeps holding me even as he picks up his book and keeps reading. I snuggle closer and let myself drift off as he reads out loud. The book is hard to follow, but it's the best bedtime story to date since it's knocking me out.

Little by little I give in until I'm out to the world.

I wake up to my alarm, alone and in bed. I huff. "Holden's sneaky."

But that's all the distraction I get until we're on the plane. I double-check the list, ask Roman for the third time if he got our certificate, then turn to Nick, since he has the list. "All the songs got to the DJ, right? And he knows about there being four first dances kind of mashed into one? And about the father-daughter dance and the multiple mother-son dances?"

"Yes," Nick says.

"Holden, my mom asked to dance with you," I say, looking at outstanding notes, but then I see Roman's handwriting. "And so did Roman's grandmother."

"Nonna took a shine to you." Roman shrugs at Holden's face.

"I'm going with Nonna." He sighs.

"Good. And we have everything for the caterer, right?" I ask Roman. "He knows about the people who requested specifics, about the baby and-"

Roman shuts me up by kissing me. I just stare at him. He winks. "Sophie, everything is set. I promise."

I look at my outstanding notes and see something that Nick put in. When I level a glare at him, he shrugs. "I think it's reasonable."

"No kissing at all once we land?" It sounds like a punishment.

"Sweetheart, we want our kisses on the altar to be special, don't we?" he asks.

That's a good point, but I don't like it. "Three days."

"Five."

"Four." I give an inch.

Nick adjusts, then crosses the private jet to take my hands. "Five and I promise to introduce my mother to yours so you don't have her asking a million questions."

"Just a million?" I pretend to think about it. I haven't met most of their families. I've only met Roman's. Even with just Holden's brother coming, I have two sets of parents to meet and I don't remember Roman's mother so I don't know how that is going to go, not to mention my mom's siblings and their families who somehow managed to get added. "Fine."

Nick kisses me, pouring all his affection into a kiss that sweeps me off my feet and makes me twice as frustrated that I lost in the compromise. He sits down and adjusts himself. At least I'm not the only one frustrated.

"The wedding night is going to be intense, isn't it?" I ask, glancing between the three men on the plane.

"Very." Holden's gaze rakes over me as if I'm already naked.

"And Gunner is arriving?"

"He will land tomorrow," Roman answers, taking my hand and kissing across my palm. "Relax, Bambina."

I point at Nick with my free hand. "Four days with Gunner."

He narrows his eyes, but gives in with a nod. "I have a feeling your brain will not be focused on kissing once we land."

I don't want to admit he's right, but deep down, I have the feeling that he is. Even though my guys have assured me over and over again that everything is taken care of, the controlling side of me says I don't know it until I've seen it.

I trust my fiancés, but the "seeing is believing" thing is very real to me. So I keep peppering them with questions until Roman rolls his eyes and shoves his tongue down my throat again.

When he releases me, Holden claims my mouth before another question can be asked. I trade-off between them, accepting the soft touches, whispered promises, the toe-curling, spine tingling kisses until there's no thought in my head.

"I wish we could join the mile-high club," I murmur, slumping back into Nick. "Are you sure that we can't just -"

"On the way home." He assures, stroking along my hip and then right along the edge of my shorts. "We're going to feed you now, then you're going to nap otherwise you're going to drop from exhaustion when we land."

I huff, but can't argue when a five-star meal is brought out. Once I shove it all down, my eyelids drop. I only managed about four hours of sleep last night–not that I'm surprised that Nick knows–and with all this stress, the things to keep in mind, the people to make happy, I'm losing my mind.

At least we got the seating chart done before we left. Once we get to the reception, it will be on our guests to talk to each other and we'll get to relax ... in theory.

We get to the hotel and that's when I find out I'm not rooming with any of my men. In fact, they have attached rooms, each with a double bed. I narrow my eyes at Nick, who just smiles.

"This is bullshit."

"Sophie." He sweeps me into his arms. "We have the marriage suite after the wedding. It's a huge room. One of those deep tubs you love, a shower, a massive bed, a little kitchen and living room area, and a view to die for. Be patient."

"My patience is gone." I hiss, then jerk him toward me and kiss him hard.

I lick into his mouth and nibble his bottom lip while grinding against him. He hardens for me and clings to me. I step back toward my room and Nick follows without question, claiming me anyway he can. When he grabs my ass and rubs himself right where I want him, I wrap a leg around him, then bite his tongue and draw back, kissing along his jaw until I get to his ear.

"Now you get to be hot and bothered until after the reception," I whisper. He groans and frustration etches into his features. I kiss his nose. "Welcome to my current level of frustration."

Roman tries to cover his obvious smirk, and Holden shakes his head. Both kiss me and promise to come get me as soon as we all get settled. When I open my door though, I see a second bed. And I see a suitcase.

I look around but don't see a single soul. I set my things on the bed, see the curtain move, then I'm jerked up and squeal against a hand that's over my mouth. I kick just before Valerie pops out.

"Surprise, Sweets." Gunner sets me down and kisses my temple. "Miss me?"

I shove him as my heart threatens to stop dead, then give him a pathetic excuse for a glare. He pulls me close and restarts my brain with a kiss that punishes me for everything I just did to Nick.

I groan and melt against him. He gives me the same boyish, excited smile. "Also, before you give me an angry talking to, I helped plan your bachelorette party. Danny has Massimo babysitting, so it's you two, Valerie, over here, and that cousin you mentioned was in your bridal party, Bailey?"

I just gape. He swats my ass hard. "Have fun …." Something dark passes over his eyes and he kisses me again, a claiming kiss that ruins any chance of me *not* being horny. "Not too much fun."

"Get out of here, old-timer," Valerie orders with a playful smile. "It's time for the girls to play."

GUNNER

The look on Sophie's face when she realized it was me was almost as good as the look she gave me after I kissed her. That hooded, hungry gaze made me hard and eager. It's a good thing Valerie was there. I know that if she hadn't been then, I wouldn't have been able to resist.

I would have thrown Sophie down and broken that damn rule that says no sex until the wedding night. Nick already told me I don't get to kiss her after tomorrow. Dick. I could kiss her every day and it would still be as intense as the first time.

All he's doing is rearing me up for a whole make-out session with an audience. But I go to the connecting rooms and flop back on the bed, I claimed. Holden looks at me and smiles. "How was the surprise?"

"She was pissed, then *very* frustrated," I smirk. "Poor thing is going to combust before we get to the altar."

"You or her?" he teases.

"Both," I groan. "Are we doing a bachelor party or are we just kicking back and getting some quality rest?"

The joining door opens and Roman and Nick come in. Nick stretches and Roman pulls a shirt over his head, having just gotten through the world's fastest shower. I sigh. "That means we're doing something."

"With Massimo and Matthew," Roman agrees. "Tonight."

"Mandatory?"

"You're the one who took the fastest option out of NY. and got here four hours ago," Nick says. "You could have come in tomorrow morning like we told Sophie."

"Then it wouldn't have been a surprise."

"We're going to a bar. Just hanging out, maybe a strip club after, but it'll be a peaceful night," Holden says.

And Holden's the one, I believe. He wouldn't lie to me about what we're doing, especially since he's not a party animal. We end up getting around and dressed before Massimo busts in, excited, with huge glasses, a bigger smile, and a shirt that says: I'm with the grooms.

I laugh at his shirt and shake my head. Matthew comes in next, wearing the same shirt in bright pink. They turn around and the shirt says, "wish the bride luck."

That breaks Holden, Nick, and Roman. Just like that, I'm up and ready to go. We head to a bar, people buy us drinks, ask us questions, give us looks, but no one comments–in English at least. I overhear a few people saying that we're full of shit or gay or gross Americans, but I don't care.

I know that in just a few days, we're going to have Sophie. And we'll have her forever. No petty comment from a stranger can compare to that. Matthew nudges me. "Everything good?"

"Yeah. Listening in since people assume none of us speak French."

With that loud comment, four people see themselves out of the bar. Matthew chuckles and buys me a shot. "I'm serious, man. All good in the penthouse?"

"It's been hella stressful, honestly. I don't know how you and Bella managed it even with a year. It's taken a whole team to get this done. If Sophie's mom was working full time, I don't think it would have happened." I admit, downing the shot. "Some fights, bickering, seeing a new side to my sweet little thing."

"Not as sweet?" Matthew chuckles. "As long as she doesn't run into an ex or something, I think you'll be fine."

"And none of my exes got invited." I chuckle. "I think we're in the clear. We just need to get to the aisle and we'll be fine. How are you and Bella?"

"She wants a baby," Matthew groans. "I mean, a part of me loves it. I want a kid and I feel ready, but damn. It's a rollercoaster already. Near constant sex when the pee stick says go, but I'm not even allowed to jerk off!"

"What?" I choke on my beer.

He goes into the pros and cons of trying for a kid. I just listen, feeling my desire to be a father dropping. Maybe, once Sophie gets there, she'll just be done with birth control and leave it to chance. I like the sound of that. Feels better than planning it out, even though I know having a plan is the best way to get a baby.

Even if at least one MTV series makes it look easy. But I know all it will take is Sophie asking to get on that kind of schedule and we'll fall in line. Not that we won't tempt her, but … it would be hard to resist if she wants something.

Roman and Massimo yell at the TV and I see a soccer game on. Some French guys cheer and I can already feel the fight brewing. I insist on us getting dinner and it helps to calm things down a little.

Only a little.

Matthew laughs and nudges Holden — shoving him into me. What happened to his alcohol tolerance? Jeeze.

"Can you believe you guys are all marrying one woman?" He chuckles. "I mean, think about where we were when we were in active duty. Roman had his girl Cheyanne back home. Gunner was engaged to what's her name?"

I flinch. "Sienna."

"And then Holden–who was that girl you were still pining over? The one that had left you when you went home for Christmas before you could pop the question?" Matthew asks.

Holden takes a long drink. "Nancy."

"And now you all fell in love with the right one. See, heartache leads you somewhere." His eyes are glassy and wild. "We need strippers."

I shake my head at him, shaking off the reminder of Sienna. The prenup drove her away, but I know that the only one that still has anything in their head for an ex might be Holden. Nancy left him when he refused to accept the discharge. Then he went and was injured so badly that he was discharged.

But she was already with someone else. He'd lost his chance. And when she had broken up with the sleazeball, Holden had been sure that she'd turned him away because of his leg. I rub his shoulder and he smiles.

"Sophie is worth it all," he says.

As if that's the only thing that needs to be said, we all down another shot, eat our steaks, potatoes, and sides, drink beer, then stumble to the first strip club the driver recommends. The girls are delicate, demure, and borderline rude, but they can smell money on us along with the alcohol and are happy to entertain considering we're at a VIP section.

The girls are fun, but I don't care to have any in my lap. Massimo looks at me like I'm crazy as two girls share his lap. Once they go to get us another round, he kicks my leg. "What the hell. I thought you were the one who likes to party!"

"Strippers don't compare to my fiancée." I shrug. "I feel bad that I can't get it up for them."

Massimo laughs and we give each other hell while drinking, smoking, and having a good time. By the time we head back, it's us grooms who are holding up our groomsmen. Matthew is close to vomiting and Massimo has reached the level of drunk where he loves everyone.

He gives me a drunk smile. "You're great." He practically slaps me instead of patting my face. He says something in Italian and Roman rolls his eyes from where he's propping Massimo up on the other side. Massimo grins. "Roman knows what I mean."

"Unfortunately."

We get into the hotel and, almost immediately, Holden freezes. Matthew falls to the ground as he stares at the check-in counter. "No."

"Hold. Help please." Nick begs as he peels Matthew off the floor. "Come on, Can't do this alone, buddy."

"She *can't* be here."

I take in the woman with springy black hair that spreads into a halo-like afro. Her olive skin, delicate curves, and big eyes. Hell, she's beautiful. Really beautiful. If she'd been at the strip club, maybe I'd have lingered just a little.

"Who?" Nick asks. "Come on, Matthew."

"The floor feels good," he argues.

"Oh, I know it does, but wouldn't it be nicer to be in a shower?"

"I like water." Matthew hiccups.

I roll my eyes and adjust my grip on Massimo. "Holden, neither of these idiots are getting lighter. Can we please get an explanation in the elevator?"

He snaps to and grabs Matthew with strength I was sure he didn't have after that many drinks. We get in the elevator and hit the button for our floor. Holden's still pale as can be, and his dark eyes are fuming.

"Speak of the devil and there she is." His voice is hoarse–a bad sign.

"Why?" Nick asks. "Who was that?"

"Nancy," he says.

The name rings a faint little bell, then Matthew lifts his head and offers some insight. "Dumb bitch lost her chance."

Holden shakes his head. "I don't know how she's here. Why? None of it."

"Does it matter?" I ask. I smack Massimo. "Wait until we get upstairs to knock out. You're a big fucker."

"You sound like my wife," he says, swiveling to look at me. "Nah. Not as sexy when mad."

"I'm hurt." I gasp. "But at least I don't have to deal with your cock."

"It's a privilege."

"Says every man," I grunt.

We drag the half-asleep men to our room and toss Matthew in the shower and Massimo on the bed. I roll out my neck and point at Holden. "Explain?"

"The one Matthew brought up. She left me because I refused to accept the discharge and went back. My brother must have mentioned something."

"Why? That was years ago. God, an entire lifetime ago," I say.

"She was close with my family. High school sweethearts. We were together for six years and my parents called her their daughter and everything." He explains. "Sophie is going to lose her shit. She was very clear about no exes. None of hers, none of ours."

"If Sienna shows up, I'm getting a fake mustache, speaking French, and getting security guards for the wedding." She was so fucking possessive, so sure I was cheating. And my jokes only set her temper off worse. If the sex hadn't been so great, if I had known that level of jealousy wasn't a compliment, then I would have been out. "I can do that for you."

"Roman?" Holden asks. "Any sign of yours?"

"I didn't look. I was busy with that idiota." He motions to his cousin.

Nick holds his hands up. "No sign of any exes from me."

I nod, then rub my forehead. "It'll be fine. I can deal with it for you, Hold."

"You already had an issue in Hawaii," Nick says.

"Yeah, with an *ex*. So if I take care of Holden's knowing that she's not interested, doesn't know me, then I can just steer her away. It'll be fine. Sophie will never know what's going on." I plan. "It's the least I can do, man. You don't need the distraction and you have a shit poker face. She'll know if something is up."

Roman looks at his phone and lets out a string of curses that don't need a caption to be understood. He squeezes his phone, then stops. "Neal is here."

"Excuse me?" Nick snorts. "What the fuck is happening?!"

A damn good question.

SOPHIE

I laugh with Valerie, Danny, and Bailey. All of us are in some stage of drunk, and I don't know if I'm more shocked that Danny seems to do the best, or that Valerie is so sloshed she kicked off her heels despite her first rule of going out being if she can't walk in her heels, she just doesn't move until she can.

"I'm serious!" Danny continues. "That bitch tried to say that I was out of line because she didn't see a flagrant foul. My son would have recognized it and he's still working on fucking object permanence."

I laugh, shoving the silly half veil from my face. I see my mom and she looks us over as I give her a ridiculous smile. She shakes her head. "Looks like you girls have had a good time."

"Danny got us free drinks all night by beating the bartender in an arm-wrestling match. Three times straight." I laugh.

"His face!" Valerie says, clutching her middle. She's complained about cramps from laughing too hard multiple times.

"Ugh. Bed. Please." Bailey begs.

"We got this. Talk to your momma," Danny says.

They half carry Bailey to the elevator and I motion to my little white dress and veil. "I think this will do."

My mom laughs. "In Vegas maybe, not here. Remember your dress?"

I stumble as I try to picture it, then bounce. "Yes! I can't wait."

"About time we see some excitement for the wedding."

Wedding. Where are my husbands? I look around. "Did the guys already come back?"

"I don't know, honey. We're just checking in."

"It's after one in the morning," I say.

"It's almost three." Mom corrects me, guiding me to the elevator. "Let's get some water into you, some food, and we're going to get a head start on the hangover cure."

"More alcohol?" I guess.

She pats my head. "You are my child. I knew it. Now tell me about your men."

"They're denying me sex." I huff. "And kisses. One more day to kiss them and then I get a lot of nothing until the wedding."

"Poor thing."

"It's been five days since any of them have slept with me and that's way too long. I have four of them! I should get laid at least daily." I cross my arms and pout. "They want it to be special or something."

"Well, that's sweet, honey. You should be happy about that."

I snort, then catch my foot on the edge of the rug and face plant on the floor. I groan, and my mom squeaks. "Sophie!"

I hear a door open, then Roman sticks his head out. I groan as I roll over on the floor. "The carpet tastes gross."

My mom rolls her eyes and tries to pull me up, but I'm next to no help, just lying there with my hand up. I hear a heavy sigh, then I'm in the air. I wrap my arms around Roman. "You're so strong."

"You're very drunk, Bambina."

"It's just fun," I hum, kissing his neck. "Are you sure you don't want to carry me to the fun room?"

"Soph."

"Please. I'm so empty."

My mom walks away while laughing. Roman stands me up and I cling to him, my body stuck on his like it should be. "I miss you."

"I know." He assures me, kissing me. "Soon."

"I don't want to wait." I complain. "I want you and Nick and Holden and Gunner all over me. It's my favorite."

He puts my veil headband back in place and lifts my chin. "Be a good girl for me, Bambina."

I bounce. "I enjoy being good for you."

"I know you do." His lips ghost across mine. "So be good and let me take you to bed. Do you remember your room number?"

"Nope." I shrug. "To yours, I go."

He chuckles and kisses me. I moan and try to climb him, eager to touch him, to lick across his sexy abs, to have his big, strong hands all over me. And he smells so good. Tobacco, bourbon, and something that's unique to Roman. Something that makes my stomach do somersaults until I feel sick.

He picks me up, giving me kisses whenever I ask. He sets me down and I see my other guys. I beam. "Yay."

"Sweets!" Gunner picks me up, and spins me until my stomach heaves. "Oh no, are you drunk?"

I pout. "And Roman won't fuck me."

"Poor thing." Gunner kisses me. "How are you supposed to survive while drunk *and* horny?"

"Fix it?" I rub myself against him, then try to find his cock with my hand.

He sets me down and holds my hands behind my back, showing me off to Nick and Holden. "Look what Roman brought us."

I giggle. "Hi."

Nick and Holden both kiss me, but Holden looks sad. I struggle against Gunner until he lets me go. I stumble into Holden and he catches me. I rub over his hard arms and shiver. "So sexy."

"Sophie."

"What's wrong?" My eyes flick to his. When I look at my other fiancés for answers, none of them seem to meet my eyes. "What don't I know? Am I going to be mad?"

"In the morning, baby. You need some sleep and sobering," Holden says before kissing me again. "Even if I like the way tequila tastes on your tongue."

"I like the sound of that. I spilled some tequila. You should lick it all up." I tug at the neck of my dress, trying to pull it down.

Holden catches my hand and then Nick sweeps me up into his arms, firefighter style. "Nope, let's go."

"But!"

"The only butt I'm interested in is yours and I can't bite it until our wedding day," he says.

I wrap my arms around his neck. "I'm so lucky."

"Yeah?"

"Four amazing men. Manly men. Sexy men. All to myself. Forever." I rub his jaw and take in his sexy blue-gray eyes. "I love you."

"Is that the tequila talking?"

I shake my head. "You're so good to me. All the time. Even when I'm bitchy. You take care of me without making me feel useless and … and I don't like this. Put me down."

"Sophia-"

"Too nauseous." I've reached the point where I know I'm drunk and hate it. I grab my stomach as Nick sets me on my feet and close my eyes as I lean against him. He holds me still for a while, then I nod. "Bed, please. I don't want you to see me throw up."

"I can handle it, sweetheart."

"It's too gross. You'll change your mind," I argue.

"Never." He kisses my cheek, my neck, anywhere he can reach anytime we have to pause. We make it to my door and my mom stands there waiting. "Can you handle this, Diana?"

"I was there in the college days," Mom says. "Ready for Gatorade and cookies, honey?"

"Yes!" I nod, but I turn and wrap my arms around Nick. "I love you. Drunk and sober."

"Not enough to let me hold your hair?"

"No." I screw my face up. "For your own protection. Breakfast tomorrow?"

"Let's plan for lunch." He kisses my nose. "Get some sleep."

But as soon as the door is closed, I walk to the bathroom, get on my knees, and vomit up everything in my stomach. I see Bailey in the shower, coming to, and nod. Next time Danny wins something, I'm not taking part. I promise myself before my stomach rolls again.

Mom takes care of us, but I know morning is going to suck the second I lie down. Danny adjusts my leg, so it's on the floor, promising it will help, then flops over and goes to sleep like it's the easiest thing in the world.

In the morning, I groan and rub my temple. I'm force-fed some kind of sausage and bacon sandwich, three extra-strength Advil, and more water than I can handle. It takes two hours for me to commit to a shower. Valerie shoves me when she decides it's her turn and I dry off before pulling on a white top and a flower printed skirt. The theme is white all the way to the wedding.

I look at the time and hit the elevator button three times, determined to meet my guys for lunch. But when the door opens up, it's not any of my fiancés there, its' Neal. He looks me over, pushes himself in, and hits all the buttons.

I can't get my brain to work before the door closes. Neal takes a deep breath. "Sophie, I couldn't not come."

"You weren't invited."

"I know, but you understand you have options. You have to see how crazy this is. I'm all about respecting choices, and if you were just a sugar baby, fine, but you're getting married! You can't marry four men. It's not legal. It's insanity," he says.

I push my fingers into my temple. "Stop shouting."

"I'm serious. Don't do this just because they're rich and you can play housewife. You're capable of so much more than pushing out babies for those old guys." We stop on a floor and he says the elevator is taken before jamming the door close button. "Just ... have you thought about this at all?"

"I love them."

"Have you been without them *at all* since they started seducing you? You were living with them from the time you arrived until now. I mean, you haven't even had a chance to see other options."

"Like you?" I hiss.

He takes a step back. "I mean ... not necessarily. I'm just trying to be a nice guy."

"Funny thing." I rub my temple in circles. "Guys who have to *say* that they're nice guys, aren't that nice. I never asked you to step in. I never asked you to fly here."

"Because you're brainwashed! They have you so wrapped up that you don't know what's what! You're smarter than this. You have to see how toxic this is."

I shove him, shove him, and get off on whatever floor this is. I'll take the fucking stairs. But Neal follows. "Just explain it to me, then."

"I *love* them." I whip around to glare at him. "I was put in close proximity sure, but they forced nothing. It's always been my choice. I don't know what gave you any other idea. Is it normal? No. But I don't care! I love them and I want them forever. That's not hard to understand."

I storm down the stairs and shove the door open, but he's right behind me. "That's bullshit. You're just afraid to be on your own. You've gotten so used to them taking care of everything that you-"

Turning, I hold my hand up, right in his face. "Shut up and *listen*. Because you're not getting it. I take care of myself just fine. I do whatever I want to do, and they make it *better*. It's called fucking compromise. I don't need to be taken care of. I don't need a hero to save me from four men I love. I just need you to leave me the fuck alone so I can get through this hangover without getting tossed out of a hotel for kicking you in the balls. Got it?"

"Well, it looks like your men have company. Maybe I'm not the only one who's noticed issues." Neal sneers before walking away.

Roman's eyes are on me. Actually, just about everyone in the lobby is staring at me, except for the girl who is touching Holden, stroking his arm, and leaning toward him like she can just have him.

Gunner jogs over and takes my hand. "Well said, Sweets."

"Who is ... what?"

"Holden's ex showed up," Gunner whispered. "Also uninvited."

"But ... But she's not on the to-do list!"

HOLDEN

This is a nightmare. I just look over Nancy as she keeps petting my arm. The only thing she's said is that she can't believe I'm alive. Apparently, she thought I died overseas. Imagine that. Then she heard I was getting married from my brother–because Aaron can't keep his fucking mouth shut–and had to see it to believe it.

And now Sophie's yelling about someone getting the fuck out of her life. I lift my head and see Neal stalking away, glaring at us. Gunner goes to Sophie and I fight the urge to do the same. She doesn't need to be overwhelmed.

Nancy strokes my arm again. "We should talk. I have so much to tell you and we need to catch up."

"I'm getting married," I say.

"I know, but ..." Her gold eyes glisten with tears. "I thought you were dead. Dead! Do you know what that did to me?"

I just stare at her. She hugs me and I keep standing there, not sure what to do. It's been over a decade since I saw her. Longer since she touched me. I've kicked her so far out of my brain that I'm not sure what to do now that she's standing right in front of me waiting for me to respond like I owe her that.

"I'm ... I'm getting married in five days, Nancy."

"You don't have to," she breathes. "You don't. Don't rush. Just talk to me, let's get everything out on the table and we can ... we can get lunch and–please, Holden. You don't know how ... how much of a miracle this is."

I close my eyes a moment. Fucking hell. This shouldn't even be a question in my head. It's an obvious no. It should be. But I don't know that I can tell her no. Not when we have the history we do.

Nick looks at me and I know he's heard everything. He nods once. When I say nothing, he shoos me. "Go. We'll take care of Sophie."

"But-"

"Please, Holden. Just one lunch. That's it. That's all I'm asking." Nancy clutches me tighter like she needs me to survive.

Have I ever been able to hurt her? Six years together and the only time I dug my heels in was when she asked me to leave my platoon and stay. It would have saved my leg, but I would have lost so much. The only time I've ever made her cry. The only time I've ever told her no without compromise.

After an unsteady breath, I nod. "Let me go."

She does as I ask, then I walk with her to the restaurant in the hotel. We sit on the veranda, the sun shining down on us. It's mid-summer, but not as hot as it feels in New York. I'm sure the ice slinking through my veins doesn't help.

Because I know Sophie is going to be hurt by this. I know it as well as I know that not fighting with Nancy means I'm going to fight with Sophie. Days before our wedding. Gunner tried to handle it, tried to step in, but Nancy is hard to stop. Her softness covers her ambition and determination well.

She orders soda water with a lime twist and I get a coffee. Because I need it. I drink it black, trying to keep a hold of myself. Nancy swallows, and orders some food. I do the same and swallow the scalding coffee before setting it down.

"You're alive," she says then laughs once. "I still can't believe it."

"I am."

"And engaged. And doing well."

I nod.

She twists a bracelet around her wrist, one I recognize. I gave it to her our first Christmas as a couple. After a slow exhale, she continues. "I heard you were in a terrible accident, and then I heard nothing. Your mom was so upset. And then I just didn't hear a word. It was like your whole family fell off the face of the earth so I just assumed the worst and because we'd broken up I just ..."

"I survived."

"And you look good. Why didn't you look me up? Why didn't you-"

"You gave me an ultimatum, Nancy," I say. "You or the military."

She sucks her bottom lip and nods. "I was young and stupid. I was twenty-one and thinking about our future. I was sure that if you stayed something bad would happen. I felt it in my gut and I ... I couldn't just sit around waiting for the news that you were gone."

"I couldn't leave my friends without me. We worked well together. We only lost two people in our platoon on that second trip."

"And you were almost one of them!" She calms herself and takes a deep breath. "And then I didn't even know you were alive."

"It was better that way."

"Did you do more tours?"

"Medical discharge," I grunt, taking another long drink.

Nancy scans me. I know I have a nasty scar just under my ear, one on my face, but nothing that would suggest the reality of what happened to me. She leans her head to the side. I pat my leg. "No one has use for a one-legged soldier."

"Oh." She nods and rubs her hands together. "I didn't even …"

"And I'm engaged," I say. "I'm in love and happy."

"But Aaron said you're sharing her. You were never the sharing type. Did that change when …" She shakes her head. "You're worth more than that, Holden. You don't have to share just because-"

I scoff and shake my head. Her eyes narrow at me. I know that I'm not as shy as I used to be. I was the nerd that felt lucky just to catch Nancy's eye as a friend. When she'd kissed me–having to make the first move–my world exploded.

But I'm not that man anymore.

"It's my choice. Sophie is good for all four of us and I'd rather share her with my best friends than not have her at all. And it works. Our dynamic is …" I try to find the words. "It's as close to perfect as I can get."

"You don't see your own worth."

"You haven't met my fiancée." I challenge.

"I don't have to! She's greedy and indecisive if she can't choose just one of you! I mean, it's only legal with one of you, obviously. Don't you want more? Don't you want a woman that just wants you? Who is more than happy to have just you?"

Her hand creeps across the table to brush my wrist. I draw back. "It's been a lifetime since we were together. We're not the same people."

"I haven't changed!"

"I have," I say. "I'm not the same confused boy I was. I don't need other people to validate me and I don't want the same things I used to. I'm happy as I am, not because I'm complacent or settling, but because every day Sophie gives me a reason to be happy. She supports me, challenges me, makes me think about things differently."

"But-"

"And I live with my best friends, men I know would die for me. We're more than friends, more than brothers. It's a relationship that few other people will understand and that's okay. I don't care because I know that this is what I want for my future. I don't have any hesitations."

"Then why even bother having lunch with me?" she asks. "If you knew that nothing I said was going to change your mind?"

"Because I will not run away from conversations that need to happen anymore." I stand, put more than enough money on the table to cover all the food. "Take my food to go and enjoy it later."

"Where are you going?!" She stands. "We're supposed to be talking for an entire lunch!"

"I need to talk to my fiancée before she can think something might happen."

"Maybe it will." Nancy rubs my hips, standing in front of me. "It could, Holden. Just run away with me. Come home with me. We can settle down in Arizona. We can have the house and life we always dreamed of."

"I told you, that's not who I am anymore, Nancy. I love New York. I love Sophia. I love my life and I wouldn't trade it for anything."

"What if I had been pregnant?"

I pause. This is a terrible hypothetical. I feel anger heat my veins. She swallows. "I thought I was. I was a month late. But when I went to the doctor, I found out it was nothing. I didn't act irrationally. I wanted you home to be a father. But when you chose … When I realized I wouldn't be enough, what was the point?"

"You weren't willing to compromise. I said one more. One more and I'd come home. You gave up on me, Nancy."

"Like you stopped me!" She yells. "You chose nightmares, PTSD, losing a leg, war itself over being with me."

"I made a commitment, and you knew, even back then, I wouldn't turn my back on a commitment. You encouraged it until you didn't."

She sniffs.

I shake my head. "It was a lifetime ago. It's better for both of us if you don't come to the wedding. Just enjoy Paris and go home."

With that, I head inside. Roman waits, sitting in the lobby. When he looks at me, he stands and I rub the back of my neck. "One fight down."

"Not civil?" he asks.

"She was expecting the old me."

"Ah, shy, silent, passive as hell, the one who looked for any kind of direction in someone else." Roman nods. He pats my shoulder. "That boy grew up fast."

"And I know what I want, Roman. I want the life we have laid out with Sophie. Nothing can tempt me away from it." Then I look around. "And she is …"

"Crying. Possibly drinking. Her mom and Valerie got her to focus on the list so she's double-checking the venues with Nick. Gunner's setting up a tasting for the meal today so we're busy."

Of course. Because Sophie is going to need to cool off and to calm down. I close my eyes a moment. "It would have been worse if I wouldn't have talked to her, right? I had to."

"You had to," Roman agrees. "It would have been sketchy, she would have kept coming up, and that would have made it look like you were hiding something. Now you know everything and you still choose Sophie."

I nod. "Without question."

Roman pats my back just before Gunner comes down and asks for a car to head to a restaurant. Gunner glances between us and relaxes back. "Well, now that's off the list."

"Sophie?" I ask him.

"She's ... upset." He confirms. "Kind of ran. I mean, after being cornered by Neal in an elevator, she-"

"What?" Roman demands through gritted teeth.

Gunner holds his hand up. "Later on that one, because we're going to rock-paper-scissors for who gets to kick *that* ass." He returns his focus to me. "She's had a long morning. Hungover, dealing with double checking things, Neal, seeing you with another girl without any kind of warning and without knowing what's going on."

"And you said what?"

"That she was your high school ex, that she left you when you got deployed again, and that was all I knew. After the shit with Bella, and Sasha, and me with the strippers, her mom all over us, I think it's just been too much on her heart."

"I made myself clear," I say. "Nancy was in love with a different me. I belong to Sophie and Sophie alone. No one else. I want no one else."

Gunner pours the champagne he brought down, hands Roman and me a glass and raises his in a toast. "Cheers to a hard conversation coming up."

"Private conversation." Because if it's not, Gunner is going to help, and this is something that I need to say for myself. "Is it just me or is this getting more complicated by the day?"

SOPHIE

*N*ick tries to get me to focus on where the altar will be, under a gorgeous tree to protect us from the sun and make for the best pictures as we walk through the garden. Valerie asks questions, taps her fingers, and makes comments, but all I can see is that damn woman.

The way Holden caved and led her away saying nothing to me. How Gunner rushed and said she was an old ex–the one that pushed him away. Well, she'd have to be stupid to push him away now.

He's a hell of a man. Understanding, kind, with such a firm grasp on his mental health, so much determination, so happy, so … lovable that she'll fall in love with him all over again at lunch.

And if there's even a shred of him that loves her back …

"Sophie," Valerie snaps her fingers in my face. "Why are you checked out?"

"Valerie, can you go over notes with Diana, please? I want to make sure we're not missing anything," Nick says.

She shrugs and walks to my mom. Nick brushes his fingers over my cheek, then his hand slips into my hair as he pulls me against his chest. I sniffle, then cry all over again. I feel like everyone's trying to tear us apart.

I'm not crazy. I know my guys have exes. They're amazing and confident and successful. If I'd allowed all their exes to show up, they'd fill the whole hotel. But knowing they exist and seeing them wrapped around my guys are two separate things.

Nick rubs my back and doesn't say anything. I get control over myself after a moment and pull back just for him to wipe my tears. "Talk to me, sweetheart."

"What if she reminds him he doesn't have to share with her? That he can just have her. He's not in the military anymore. They could have a life and … and …"

"You've seen how much he's grown just by knowing you, Sophie. He's dedicated to counseling, hasn't been having nightmares, and has opened up. It's because of you, sweetheart. He's a changed man because of you, Sophie. He loves you."

"Yeah, so I'm just an addition to therapy."

"It's because he loves you and he wants you to know it. He's pushing himself to give you everything he can so *you* don't leave *him*. He loves you as much as I do. As much as Roman does. As much as Gunner does."

I nod and lean into Nick's hand. "I'm just being emotional and crazy, aren't I?"

"I don't know." He smiles. "I've considered texting my ex to come give me hell, so you'll fight for me, too."

"I fight for you every fucking day." I stamp my foot. "Hell, I'm glad I don't know French because I've seen so many girls give you longing looks. I've seen them whisper to each other while pointing at you.

Each of you is a catch and I guess I just have to accept that women will always want you. All of you."

"Sucks to be them." He kisses my forehead, then looks around. "Come on."

"Where are we-" I ask.

But he drags me through the gardens, then shows me a beautiful flower arrangement, like a painting. I put a hand to my chest as I take it in, but before I have it committed to memory, Nick leads me to a bridge. When we look out over the water, I see they've placed stones to mimic one of Monet's paintings.

Nick stands behind me, his arms keeping me close as we look at the water together. He rubs my shoulders, then kisses my neck. "I think each of us should take pictures with you separately and together. I want to take a picture with you here, just like this."

My throat is all scratchy with emotion and he's not helping. "And, at some point, you and I are painting. We've talked about it so much, but we've never found the time. We're doing it. And then we're going to Louvre so I can show you the things that made me want to paint to begin with."

"Nick," I whimper.

"Because I want you to know everything about me, Sophie. I want to share everything I love with you. Art, being in nature, even staring at clouds and finding shapes. We could find a hobby to start together– like photography or growing plants. I don't care what it is, I'm willing to give everything a shot. You're worth so much to me."

I turn in his arms and stand on my toes. Nick fits his mouth to mine and kisses me. Stars burst behind my closed eyes and the embers set me on fire as our tongues tease and tangle. He knots his hand in my hair, and I can feel his heart fluttering in his chest.

When he draws back, I bite my lip. "We broke a rule."

"One of my favorite things about you," he whispers. "Is that you never let a rule stand in the way when you're passionate. You are full of life, Sophie. You make me feel capable of everything that I want to try."

"Bungee jumping?" I ask.

"Let's do it right—over the Grand Canyon," he says with a smile.

"Cage diving with great whites?" I laugh.

"Why not? I swam with sharks before." He shrugs. I gape and he laughs. "I didn't tell you that story?"

"No!" I bump his hip. "You keep managing to keep secrets."

"I fed bull sharks off the coast," he says, leading me back through the garden. "I was supposed to go on a trip to watch great whites breaching, but decided to go and kayak in Alaska to see the orcas instead."

"Did you know that orcas have been attacking great whites for the livers?" I bounce on my toes.

We go back and forth about shark facts, which keep us busy, especially when we join Valerie and she includes her own stories until we get to the reception hall. Of course, I see Holden, Roman, and Gunner there, too.

Tears prick my eyes again and I take an unsteady breath. Nick kisses my temple. "Go talk to him and I'll reward you."

"Bribery?" I snort.

"I may or may not have a picture that I drew as a kid … of a shark," he whispers in my ear with a chuckle.

I groan, kiss his cheek, then take a hesitant step across the room. It feels so big. I can't think of crossing it alone, but Holden meets me halfway and hugs me so tight that I think my spine realigns. Without a word, he takes my hand and leads me into a hallway where we have some privacy.

"Sophie, I'm so sorry."

"I know you had to." I rub my arm. "But I … it doesn't mean I like it."

"I didn't plan it." He assures me, trying to calm me. He looks at my face and shakes his head. "Oh, baby, I made you cry."

"I just have to accept that you guys are girl magnets."

"I told her no. She wanted to try again, tried to say that you're greedy and making me share because you make me feel like I'm not good enough to have you to myself and that's not true."

I wipe at my eyes.

Holden hugs me again after a brief hesitation. "Fuck, I love you so much. As soon as I sat down, I wanted to get up and go to you. As soon as she said she wanted one lunch to change my mind, I knew that there was no point in the conversation."

I sniffle. "You loved her once, though."

"So long ago. And it was a different me. You make me want to be so much better. Constant inspiration." He insists. "She could be the most beautiful, the most successful, richest woman in the world, and it wouldn't matter."

"Why?"

"Because she's not you, Sophie." He lifts my chin and presses his forehead to mine. I can tell he's panting, that his eyes are watering. "Please don't call this off because I had a meal with her. I told her no. I told her not to come. I told her to go home and get back to her life."

I kiss him. He freezes a moment, but then he kisses me back, his mouth so soft, so compliant, and warm and perfect. Kissing Holden is … is as good as a top-tier spa package. It has the same effect on my body. My shoulders relax and every muscle relaxes.

"I'm yours," he breathes before kissing me again. "Completely and totally. Unashamed."

"Even if you're sharing me?"

"You're sharing me too." He chuckles, kissing my forehead. "We both love the guys. Granted, I don't want to fuck them, but I'm so happy at the idea of us all living together. I love our game nights. I love our group dates. I love the idea of a future where we all travel together, where I know they love you as much as I do. Where we're all happy."

I wipe at my eyes again and Holden curses. "Fuck, I'm sorry. I'm supposed to be fixing the tears."

Rolling my eyes, I shove him. "Save that shit for the vows."

He hugs me and rubs his fingers through my hair. "Don't you worry. Those are all set to go. We just have to get there."

"No more drama," I tell him.

"I'd say 'I promise', but I never would have expected Nancy to appear." He sighs. "All I can tell you is I'm not going anywhere, baby."

I squeeze him and we stand there for a while, calming each other with soft touches and whispered promises. When we walk back in, I'm still a damp mess. Gunner looks between us. "Are we ... are we good?"

"Yeah." I laugh once, lacing my fingers through Holden's fingers. "We're all set. We just need to get to the wedding part of this trip."

Roman nods. Nick winks at me and we finish checking off our list for the day. The next day, I get to a salon since we didn't get that done before we left. I get a nice hair treatment, get waxed all over, get nice acrylics for the wedding, and another massage that I didn't even realize I needed.

By the time we leave, I have that brand-new feeling again. Two more days.

But the next day brings up more issues. Thankfully, no issues between the guys and exes, but Neal has taken his concerns to my dad. Because of course, he has. The asshole. Dad threatens his job, and Neal promises that this isn't over.

Gunner flexes his French at the front desk and then has Neal removed from the property. Gunner waves and I kiss his cheek. He wraps an arm around my shoulders. "I'm still mad I lost the rock-paper-scissors."

"What do you mean?"

"I wanted to kick him in the balls." Gunner shrugs. "I'm an old-fashioned man like that. A guy tries to upset my girl and I have to defend her honor."

I laugh. "Oh, that kind of old-fashioned."

He grins a wide smile. "The classy kind."

I giggle and we get back to making sure everyone who is supposed to be here is checked in. The rehearsal dinner, which is more of a pre-party, is all set up for tomorrow, and I think we're going to make it. We just have to make it through two more nights and one more event.

Gunner grabs my ass, making me jump as he tries to stop his smirk. I swat his chest and he jerks me against him. "Two more nights without you, Sweets."

Oh, the promise in his eyes is going to get me through it just fine, because I know what's waiting for me.

NICK

I toss and turn in bed. I think this is the longest I've gone without sharing a bed with Sophie since that became a normal event. It's killing me. It felt good calming her down today. It felt good being open and honest about how I feel and having her do the same.

Especially considering where we were. Then all her shark facts, how excited she got when we were talking–so happy and invested that she forgot all about being upset. I smile, then pull out my phone.

I text her, letting her know how hard it is to sleep without her. Her reply is almost instantaneous. She asks why we're following that rule when we already broke one. She even offers just sleep, no sex, and promises she can control herself, but I have to turn her down, even though it kills me.

Soon enough, I'll have her in my arms and only have to let her go for work or to share her with the guys. She'll be happy and won't have to sleep in her own bed if she doesn't want to. I text her that and wish her goodnight.

In the morning, we get dressed, and go over a few logistics, including the estimated cost, even though we don't know how much Sophie's dress was. As we're getting into how we will divide everything up since Roman took care of all the deposits, there's a knock on the door.

I get up and open the door. Miles nods at me. "Nick."

"Miles."

"I wanted to ask how much I'm looking at."

All of us look at him as he snatches the paper from Roman. He nods, pockets it, and heads out. I arch an eyebrow. "Excuse us."

"We aren't asking you to pay for anything, Miles," Roman says.

"We can afford it, which you should know since you have access to payroll," Gunner teases. "Unless you dropped our pay." He chuckles.

Miles points at him. "I should, since you're getting sassy."

Gunner just grins.

"It's a tradition that I help with the wedding. I'm paying at least half."

"Take care of the dress and call it good." Holden barters.

"I pay half or I'm chipping in on the Honeymoon, which means putting money in Sophie's account whether or not she uses it," he says. "She's my only child. I will not get another opportunity to do this."

"You could pay for a party for you and Diana," Gunner says. "I mean, I'm sure she'd love that."

"She said no to anything beyond friends." He waves that away. "I'm serious. Half or …"

"Sophie won't like having a sudden increase in her account," I murmur. "Fine, Miles."

He nods and we look over the paper together. He won't tell us the price of the dress that he's already paid for, alterations and all. He clears his throat as he goes over everything, and I know it has nothing to do with the price.

Miles rubs his forehead. "I can't believe my little girl is getting married."

Roman rubs his shoulder and Miles's face goes red. He sniffs once and shakes his head. "I haven't even seen the dress or her in it and I'm tearing up."

"Hopefully, you've been doing your exercises. You have to make it up the aisle four times." Gunner chuckles. "We'll get a good picture of you."

"And I'm still considering not giving her to you." Miles snorts.

Gunner makes a frustrated sound and we keep talking finances until we get lunch. Apparently, Sophie is doing her last fitting and going over a few things, so we don't get to see her until the rehearsal dinner.

We have it in the hotel's restaurant since the venue for the reception is being used tonight. Sophie comes in wearing a little white dress. The gauzy fabric wraps around her with only one shoulder covered and when it catches the light, it glitters. Her hair is pinned, so it only falls down one shoulder and she looks like she's glowing.

She sits between the four of us, but kisses each of our cheeks before taking her spot. As expected, Roman is on her right and I've been lucky enough to snare her left for tonight. Holden and I already agreed to switch for tomorrow, but I have a feeling we're going to be rotating seats.

I see Nonna, Massimo, Danny, and a woman I don't recognize sitting together. I lean past Sophie. "Roman?"

"My mom," he says. "Giana."

I nod. Sophie asks about my parents and I point them out. "My dad is Daniel. Mom's name is Loretta."

I see her make a note. She puts down my dad has a faded dragon tattoo on his forearm and that my mom likes blue eyeshadow. I chuckle and kiss her cheek. "They loved the eighties."

Sophie giggles and rubs my thigh. "Tomorrow night, I'm demanding cuddles from everyone."

"At the same time?"

"Yes," she says, not bothering to elaborate.

I smile to myself. Holden points out his brother, and considering how similar they look, there's no mistaking Aaron for anyone else. His head is shaved, and he looks older than the last time I saw him.

Before she can ask Gunner, he's up and hugging his mother. She squeals and pinches his cheeks and he glows, thrilled with the attention. His father pats his back, his long hair back in a braid. His face reddens, and he moves his glasses to wipe his eyes.

They get sappy, but then Gunner has his sisters to deal with. I don't remember their names, so I can't help Sophie, but she watches with obvious love. "I don't know why he hides his sweet side," she says.

"I'm sure he had a reason at one time." I rub the inside of her knee and her pen drops as she looks at me. A blush fills her cheeks as I keep doodling circles there. She shivers. "I'm as impatient as you are, sweetheart."

"Sure we can't just do it tonight and party tomorrow? We're going to be so tired; we should move everything forward a day."

"Absolutely not," Roman says, then kisses her jaw. He says something in Italian and Sophie bites her bottom lip as her thighs trap my hand between them. She nods, and he grins. "Good girl," He tells her.

"Tease." She huffs.

The first course is served and Miles stands. "I want to take a moment and thank all the families for coming tonight. While this is unconventional, one thing I'm sure of is that this is a relationship that will last. I've known these four men for so long and I know no one can take better care of my daughter than they can. Fierce in battle, but caring and gentle where it counts. I know they will have a wonderful future ahead of them, despite what people may think or assume."

Sophie bursts into a huge smile and I take her hand and kiss her knuckle. "Forever."

We dig into the food, then I take Sophie's hand as we wait for the second course. "I'm first."

"Okay." She clings to me. "What if they don't like me?"

"How could anyone not like you, sweetheart?"

"Ask Sasha, I guess?" she grumbles.

But as soon as I introduce her to my mother, my mom jerks Sophie into her arms, then she steps back and holds her face between those long red nails. "You're so beautiful. Nicky, how did you get so lucky? Classy, beautiful, and smart."

My dad is a little more aloof. He looks Sophie over and shakes her hand. "Daniel."

"Sophie." She backs against me and I wrap an arm around her. "It's very nice to meet you both. Nick is ... amazing, honestly. I can't imagine not having him in my life."

"Not enough to only be with him." My dad huffs.

"Dad." I narrow my eyes. "Don't start."

He holds his hands up. "As long as you're happy and don't care about the whispers, I guess."

"Come on, honey. We met at Woodstock and that wasn't an exclusive affair," my mom teases.

My dad clears his throat, nods, and welcomes Sophie to the family in a better way. Roman takes over next, introducing Sophie to his mother. When Sophie speaks to her in Italian, Giana lights up and so does Nonna. They gush over her and Roman beams, pride radiating from him.

Sophie laughs and pats his chest, saying something in slow Italian that Roman corrects before kissing her palm. I rub Holden's shoulder. "Everything good?"

"Yeah. No sign of crashers so far," he mumbles.

"Nervous about introducing her to Aaron?"

"I'm nervous. Aaron told my parents he was invited and they'll attend tomorrow." He sighs. "I don't want them giving Sophie shit."

"Don't worry, my dad took care of that right away." I chuckle. "Mom, put him in his place."

"Did she bring up Woodstock again?"

Holden and I both laugh before I take my seat. Gunner shakes his head. "Sophie's not ready for Lucy and Hallie. If she thinks I'm wild …"

"Well, maybe they can come to visit more and Sophie will have some female friends to go out with," I suggest.

Gunner slugs me. I rub my shoulder. "Are you drunk already?"

"High on happiness." He admits, then his huge smile reappears. "I kept expecting something to stop the wedding. I was sure some kind of shit would hit the fan and we wouldn't even get here."

Roman sits down and I see Holden introducing Sophie to Aaron. They talk for a while and Sophie nods a few times and leaves with a smile. She presses a quick kiss to Holden's mouth and gives a little wave as she walks toward me and Gunner.

She shrugs, then takes a deep breath as she walks behind us, resting a hand on my shoulder. "Okay, Gun. I'm ready."

"Are you sure, Sweets?" He tugs her into his lap. "Ready to be hugged, asked a million questions, make my dad cry, and everything in between?"

She giggles and pats his chest. "Well, I can't handle them like I handle you, but I'll survive."

Gunner picks her up, making her squeal, and drags her over to the most talkative area of the room. I shake my head and Roman chuckles. "She's been swallowed by the group."

"Did Nonna understand what's going on?"

He nods, then chuckles. "She was worried I was the one marrying all of you and had a number of questions."

I laugh and feel the last of the worry roll off my shoulders.

Sophie sits back down after having to untangle herself from Gunner's family for the second course. Just as she sits, the doors open and there's Neal. He's drunk, furious, and has some kind of renewed confidence in his arguing abilities.

Miles stands first. "We already talked about this, Neal. Leave or you're have to find a new job."

"I just think there's someone Sophie may want to talk to before going through with this wedding."

I look at Sophie, confused. She straightens her back and lifts her chin. That look in her eyes is deadly, a more lethal version of Roman's domineering glare that silences rooms. She folds her fingers together.

Neal motions to someone and a handsome guy walks in. I can admit he's handsome. He looks like an all-American athlete. Sophie schools her features into a cool indifference, but I catch her biting the inside of her cheek.

Valerie coughs up a lung as she spews champagne everywhere. She manages to half swallow, but her voice still comes out. "Tristan?"

"Hey, sis." His eyes look to Sophie. "No invite?"

Neal grins a victorious smile, but I'm just fucking confused. Who the hell is this?

SOPHIA

I don't know how Neal dug up Tristan. He and I had been friends for a long time before I tried to take my shot my freshman year of undergrad. He told me we were better friends than we could ever be together. It launched a fight with Valerie that cooled off, but Tristan and I weren't the same. He graduated later that year and our conversations after were just holiday greetings and occasional catch-ups on life.

But Valerie told me all about his polyamorous relationship, how it hit a bad wall, how badly it hurt him. And then she showed me the very successful blog he's been running. A positive mental health podcaster and professor of sociology, he's done well for himself and he still looks good.

He shares Valerie's dark hair, but his eyes are a soft gray, his skin all tan, his jaw squared, and I can't stop the smile as I stand and walk toward him. He gives in, the corner of his mouth lifting.

"You did a lot better than me."

I hug him tight, sighing. "It's so good to see you."

I see Neal balk, but then he shakes his head. "Tell them, Tristan. About how this kind of relationship isn't stable. How it can't last. How people aren't made for this bullshit."

Tristan ignores him and spins me in a circle. "You grew up. Look at all this style."

I laugh, then tug him over to meet my fiancés. "Tristan, this is Gunner, Nick, Roman, and Holden, my amazing fiancés–husbands as of tomorrow."

Tristan shakes each of their hands. "Congratulations. I wish you all the best. Hopefully, Sophie hasn't been giving you guys a rough time. Sometimes she's too ambitious or wound too tight for her own good." He chuckles.

Gunner laughs. "It's four versus one there. We have the upper hand."

I look at Nick and his face softens. "She's perfect for us. Even with her temper."

Roman reaches for my hand and I squeeze his and Holden's. "I'm going to talk to Tristan a moment and then we can figure out where to put him at the reception, if that's okay with you guys."

"Of course," Holden assures. Tristan heads to the door, and Holden's eyes bounce between us. "An ex?"

"I asked him out. He said we were better as friends, and I think he wanted to avoid issues with Valerie."

Gunner nods. "Yeah, she's not one to upset."

"I promise, I'll be right back, and we can keep celebrating." Then I look at Neal. "Hey Gunner, remember that talk we had about being old-fashioned?"

A wicked grin spreads over his face.

I walk out of the room and Tristan hugs me again. "Four guys? How's that working?"

"Better than your relationship did based on what Valerie said. I know it's crazy, but we love each other. We've talked about it over and over and they only want me. It's not like I can choose when they're so good in so many ways. I wouldn't be here if-"

"Sophie, just because it didn't work for me, doesn't mean it doesn't work." He covers my mouth. "You know when it's right. If there's no jealousy, no infighting, nothing that is a red flag–and, trust me, Val would have made that clear–then go for it."

I bounce and hug him. He laughs. "I don't know why that dick paid for me to come over here, but I'm not complaining."

"I guess he only skimmed your article and assumed you'd condemn the wedding or something." I kiss his cheek. "I'm glad you're here. I thought about inviting you, but we haven't talked in so long and …"

"Adult problems." He winks. "Is there a spot by your parents?"

I lead him back inside, introduce him to my parents, and warn him to watch out for my mom. He chuckles, but as Neal continues his drunken bitching, it's Nick that gets up. Gunner has his hands ready for rock paper scissors but the fury in Nick's eyes is unmatched.

He stalks toward Neal, connects his fist to Neal's jaw, and sends him reeling backward. I go to him and pat his chest, then take his fist in my hand. It's already red.

Nick pulls me toward him and we sit down as if nothing happened. Roman calls security and then Neal is gone, even if he's whimpering and trying to explain that he was just hit. Gunner complains about not being the one to do the job, but the rest of dinner goes well.

After the last course, music plays over the speakers and I see some people dancing, others mingling, it's amazing how easily our families come together. Nick rubs my back and I lean toward him.

"That was a great punch. I almost forgot that you're a combat pro." I gush.

"How did you deal with that?"

"Because you're so gentle with me, and you help me handle problems like Neal." I kiss the hollow under his ear. "I love you, Nick. And I need you as much as I need any of the guys we live with. My world wouldn't be anywhere near as bright or beautiful without you in it."

He takes a staggering breath and pecks my lips.

"Rule breaking?" Roman's voice rumbles through me.

Nick winks and gets up to introduce his family to Gunner's. I look at Roman. "Are you upset, or angry it's not with you?"

"Neither." He pulls me up to dance with him. I laugh as he spins me under his arm. "I know the other guys don't care that I'm the husband on paper..." But he pulls me all the way against his chest. "I do. It means so much to me."

I kiss his chest since he's still holding his face out of reach. "We can always break a different rule."

I feel his laughter against my hands. "Oh no. You have to wait for me until tomorrow."

Frustration fills my chest, but I force myself to deal with it. Roman strokes his thumb across my jaw. "No complaining this time?"

"You're worth the wait. All four of you are. And I know that I'm the luckiest woman in the world. Even though I'm greedy for our future, I know that I'll miss out on the fun if I keep trying to make it come faster."

"Is that some personal growth I hear?" Gunner asks before Roman takes my hand and then spins me out to him. Gunner catches me. "Tomorrow, Sweets."

"Tomorrow." I repeat.

"I'm going to be sappy, so I hope you're prepared."

"I'm always prepared for you, Gunner. Especially that sweet and vulnerable side you save for me," I whisper in his ear.

He dips me back and heat fills his eyes. "Teasing me with a good time?"

"Every time with you is a good time." I laugh.

"God Sophie, you are the only woman for me. I think I knew it the moment I laid eyes on you." His hips brush mine and I bite my lip.

"No drinking after dinner for you, Sweets. I want you sober." His fingertips dance along my back, making me shiver. "Sober, responsive, and begging for more."

I giggle and find myself passed off to Nick. "Hello, gorgeous." He winks.

"Is Roman mad about the kiss he saw?" I ask.

"Nope. I think everyone's happy right now. Except Neal, wherever he is." I roll my eyes. I stroke over his biceps. "And you are swoon-worthy."

"So you like violence, huh?" He twists me in his arms so my back is to his chest. "I guess we'll have to spar again."

"Yes please," I pant. "Especially if it means having your arms around me."

He kisses my neck and we talk about his parents before I'm passed to Holden. He clutches me tight as he searches my eyes. He doesn't ask me if we're okay. He doesn't ask me anything. We just dance, watching each other as we move.

As the song ends, he pulls my arms around his neck. "I'm saving all my big words for tomorrow."

"Can I have a few small ones for tonight? Before Valerie steals me away?"

"I love you, baby."

"Those are plenty big." I rest my forehead against his shoulder. "I love you too. Promise me something?"

"Just about anything."

"That you guys will never make me sleep in my bed again."

Holden guides my chin up. "I promise, the next time you fall asleep on me, I'll carry you to my bed and I won't let you go until breakfast."

I hug him and promise that tomorrow will be perfect, no matter what happens before Valerie pulls me away.

"Come on, you need so much beauty rest to shake off the stress, and we're getting started early," she says.

I wave and thank everyone for coming, even though I'd rather stay right here, basking in all the warmth and love in the room. Tristan follows and I make sure he gets a room. The hotel staff is all too happy to help.

Valerie nudges her brother. "Such a party crasher. You never change."

"Eh, I still have some growing up to do. Who would have believed Sophie's the first of the three of us to get married." He chuckles.

"Um, everyone?" Valerie huffed. "I'm not the marriage type."

Her phone buzzes and I see her eyes flick toward the elevator. Tristan arches his eyebrow at me and Valerie elbows me hard, not that it stops me. "Which of the three are texting you?"

"Three? We have another multi-men situation going on?" Tristan gasps. "My baby sister!"

"Shut up. Both of you. Just because one man is texting me, doesn't mean anything's going to happen. Its all been PG."

Tristan and I gang up on her, just staring. She groans. "So it's been R with pictures that ride the NC-17 line. But he–any of them–which–

ever one I'm texting–hasn't seen the goods."

"No wonder she's rushing you to bed instead of demanding a poker and beer night. She's going to get laid." Tristan grins. "And if you're fucking, I get to know a name at least."

I leave them to bicker in the hallway and get through a relaxing shower, lotion as much of my body as possible so I'm all soft and touchable tomorrow, do a face mask, and I'm kicking back with wine when Valerie comes in.

"Which one?" I ask.

"No."

"I'm the bride. Which one?" I demand.

She rubs her toes over her calf. "I didn't mean it when I said *one*. It was just one of them texting right now."

I finish my wine. "As if I'm going to judge. You and Leif had some cute moments."

"Yeah and Hunter is an asshole which I kinda like and Chase is … something." She sits on the bed next to me. "I don't know. It feels silly like I'm just copying you."

"Those three men are nothing like mine. Well … Hunter is something like Gunner."

"Not the Gunner I've seen. He's all sweet and harmless around you," she grumbles.

I shrug. "It takes time to open up to people. Sometimes sex can do it, and you deserve to get laid taking on all these Maid of Honor duties. Why don't you go see them?"

"Because I'm as off-limits as you are … until tomorrow."

We laugh together and curl up, ignoring the second bed. Even with the hardships of wedding planning, this entire experience has been like a birthday wish on steroids. I've gotten close with Valerie all over again. I've gotten to meet almost all my fiancés' parents, I'm getting married, and tomorrow I'll be able to love on my men, all of them, for the first time in two weeks.

I look at my engagement rings and my dress hanging up in the room. Who cares about Princesses, whatever I am is so much better.

ROMAN

I adjust my tie and hear the photographer take a picture. There are two on the team and they're determined to get shots of us getting ready. But he's told us to ignore him as we get ready. Gunner laughs and shoves Nick.

"You're full of shit."

"And you're full of alcohol." He steals Gunner's glass and takes a drink.

Holden pats his shirt down as he comes out and Massimo helps him with his shoes, more than willing to be involved. I grin. "Feel like Cinderella, Holden?"

He flips me off and I grin. Today is the day. Sophia, forever. This is a day worth remembering. I pat Gunner and Nick on the shoulder. "Are you guys ready for this?"

"I don't know how to be ready for anything with her." Nick shakes his head. "She's …"

We all nod. He doesn't need to finish the sentence. We have plenty of adjectives for Sophia, plenty of memories with her, and no words are enough to describe her. I take an unsteady breath.

"I'm going last," I say.

"It'll throw her for a loop." Gunner laughs. "I can't believe you guys are trusting me to go first." His eyes go a little misty and he rubs his chest. "It means a lot."

"Gunner, Nick, Holden, then Roman." Massimo lists. "And I'll get to see her face every time. And yours." He looks at the photographer. "Please tell me you're going to get them ugly crying. I need it for posterity. Even if you don't give them the pictures."

He nods and Massimo flashes a thumbs up.

Danny comes in after a minute, holding their baby son in her arms, dressed in a little tuxedo as he cries. Gunner puts a hand to his ear. "Whoa. That's some ugly crying."

"He's very upset about his socks," Danny grumbles then holds the baby in front of her. "Listen here, Gio. You better behave."

"Oh, let him cry," Massimo soothes, gently pulling his son from Danny's arms. He bounces him a little. "It's a big day. So much is different. So many changes and people. It's all too much, isn't it?"

Gio calms a little and tugs on Massimo's tie. He beams. "There you go. See, Papá makes it all better."

Danny rolls her eyes but moves toward her husband and child. She has a robe on and Massimo's eyes heat. "Tesoro…"

"Don't start," she grumbles despite her blush. She strokes her baby's foot. "Have you told the guys yet?"

"Told us what?" Gunner pipes up.

Massimo hands me Gio and I adjust him in my arms so he can look around while I support his head. He looks at me while sucking his fingers and smiles a little, all the tears forgotten.

"We'd like you to be the godparents. You all and Sophie." Danny without her bite is hardly recognizable.

"Really?" Nick beams. "We're happy to do it."

Gunner and Holden look nervous. I know neither of them have been around babies, but it's a humbling request. I nod and thank Mass in Italian. Gio squirms in my arms and fusses, but Nick takes over.

Nick, one of the best hand to hand combat experts I've ever met is so gentle with a baby. He makes stupid faces until Gio laughs and kicks his feet. Danny's shoulders slump forward. "Thank goodness."

"Tesoro, you're so good with him. What's wrong?"

"Let's say that the bridal prep is a lot less demanding than this and leave it at that." But Danny shifts. "And he's not hungry which is … frustrating."

"So proud of you." Massimo lifts her chin and kisses her softly. "Not cursing in front of our little man."

I know the photographer is eating this up. Nick shows Gunner how to hold the baby and Gunner adjusts his arms. Gio and Gunner look at one another with confusion, like both are waiting for the other to cry.

Gunner bounces a little and the threat of tears is pushed back again. Gio squirms and Gunner adjusts. I can't help my smile. "Look at that."

"He's a natural," Nick agrees.

"Shut it. I'm not kid friendly," Then to Gio, he says, "don't let this secret out. It's just us that know I can handle this."

But after a little more time talking and calming the baby, he starts fussing and crying. Even in Massimo's arms he screams and wails. Holden takes a shot in one go and Gunner takes a few steps back before Danny picks up her child and arches an eyebrow.

"Yeah, Papá says you can cry, but that's no good." She doesn't do any baby talk, which shouldn't surprise me considering I've met the woman, but her eyes remain soft. "I know the world is scary and big, but screaming doesn't do the job."

She looks around. "Bathroom?"

Massimo leads her away and Gunner shivers. "Mildly terrifying."

"Hold, you didn't want to touch the baby?" Nick asks.

"Babies don't like me." He shrugs. "Which is fine. If I'm not confident, they'll know, and that bothers me…"

"You're thinking of snakes or dogs or something," Gunner says, slinging his arm over Holden's shoulder. "But it's fine, we'll be the fun parents and let those two do all the diaper changing and discipline stuff."

I roll my eyes, but I can't quite stop my smile.

The photographer steps in and poses us, has us drinking together, smiling, looking all serious while smoking cigars—once Danny's left with the baby—and taking pictures of us one at a time.

We go to a part of the garden and snap even more photos, dealing with the wind, the high pollen count, and everything in between. Then Sophia's dad comes up. He shakes his head. "This is the easy part."

We pose with him, and he stands with each of us. Sophia's mom joins as well. Then Miles and Diana get some pictures together. The photographer gets a text and nods. "Alright … the bride is ready."

"Fuck." Miles rubs at his face.

I pat his shoulder and Holden does the same. He takes an unsteady breath. "I don't know if I'm ready to let her go. I feel like I just got her back."

"And she'll be living in the same spot." Gunner assures him, his eyes warm. "We can set up weekly dinners, or dinners every other week. Nothing is getting rushed."

"Except the wedding." He glances between us. "Any reason?"

"We already talked about that," Nick says. "She's not pregnant."

"She better not be with the way she throws back alcohol." Diana laughs, then rubs down my chest. "Although, I could believe-"

"Diana!" Miles barks. "Please, dear."

She pouts at me, but then strokes my face. "Be good to my little girl, Roman."

She repeats the same line to each of us before dragging Miles away. I can feel my love, affection, and nervousness filling me up. I straighten my tie for the fifth time, then Nick comes over and adjusts my sleeves so the powder blue is showing again.

"Starting to feel things?" he asks.

I nod. "Not just for Sophia."

The guys and I sit on a bench in front of one of the ponds. "We've been through so much together. War, starting a business, losses and wins, and now we're going into a forever together."

Nick pats my knee. "Would you have it any other way?"

I shake my head. Gunner's eyes are misty. He takes my hand. "All those times I said I love you … they're real. I love all of you guys. Sophie is amazing and sexy and wonderful, but having you guys with me just makes everything feel right."

Nick nods. "It's hard to explain it. Lord knows my parents have asked."

"More than brothers and more than friends," Holden murmurs. "Not quite lovers."

We all laugh, but the threat of tears is still there. Gunner looks up, blinking, just like I'm sure Sophia is going to do multiple times over. "God, we don't even have makeup to worry about," Gunner says.

"Poor Sophie." Nick sighs. "Hopefully she got the waterproof type."

We joke around for a while longer, hanging out, taking photos, silly, serious, and everything in between. Massimo regains his son after about thirty minutes from a frazzled-looking Danny.

But damn she looks good. All of us stare at her, the lavender dress, accentuating her curves without being too sexy or too revealing. Her hair is organized, classy, and the makeup makes each of her features soft.

Massimo just gapes. Danny pants. "Please, Mass, take him so we can get some pictures? It'll be fast."

He sweeps his son into one enormous arm, then his other locks around Danny's waist. "You're going to get kicked out of the wedding looking like this."

"Stop." She blushes.

"So beautiful, sexy, and all mine, Tesora," he keeps purring compliments until she wraps her hand around the back of his neck. He grins. "I'm so glad you took a chance on me."

She sniffs. "Still so smooth with your words."

He kisses her without letting his son fall. When they draw back from each other, Danny rubs his arm, checks Gio, and takes a deep breath. She looks at us and puts her hands over Gio's ears.

"You all are fucked. Royally. Miles hasn't even seen her yet, but ... be ready."

With that, she kisses her baby and her husband again before dashing off, the dress held up in her hands. Massimo whistles and she flips him off. He shakes his head. "The wedding is just the start."

"What?" Gunner asks.

"When you see her coming up the aisle, you'll be sure that it's impossible to love Sophie anymore than you do right then and there. She'll read the vows and your heart will have to grow to take in all that affection, but once the wedding is done, the honeymoon is over, and you get to see your wife at her best, her worst, on the days that she feels like crap but still wants you to know she loves you … it's something else," Massimo says with a look of admiration.

I swallow that knowledge and look over to where I know they're getting ready. Sophia's been teasing us in white all week, she's been pushing the limits on kissing and sex. She's survived exes, her dad discovering us, our fights and bickering, she's survived the stress of getting a whole wedding ready in just six weeks.

How is there more to her we haven't seen? How is there possibly more of her to love? Nick clears his throat. "I think he's right. We won't be focused on seducing her and proving ourselves anymore, not once we have her. Which means we'll just be who we are. And she will too."

Gunner adjusts the watch around his wrist and I see the flair of pink that matches his tie. "We're going to start using up our PTO. I have a feeling leaving her in the morning is going to be harder." Gunner chuckles.

Holden nods, the cool orange of his tie contrasting against his skin as he fiddles with it. "It's Sophie. She's never hidden who she is." But he swallows and looks at us. "Ready for this? Really?"

All of us nod, then hold still a moment. I clear my throat. "We're not running away from her or each other. Let's promise right now. We're in this forever."

"As long as we all shall live," Holden agrees.

"Let's go!" The photographer motions us back to where we got ready. "We have a few more things to do before we line up at the altar. It's time."

Finally, it's time. We made it.

SOPHIE

I look over my dress again, the gorgeous layers, the way it hugs my body, the gauzy sleeves that brush my arm without holding on. My auburn hair has been curled, then collected to fall right down my back with only a few locks there to frame my face. My face looks fresh and dewy. I feel more like a woodland nymph than a princess.

My makeup is a good mix of dark and soft. Valerie gives me the necklace she's worn as long as I've known her, and then my mom gives me the necklace I brought. They help me put my jewelry on, and then, being silly, Valerie snaps the garter and drops to her knees.

"Just so the guys know, I had my hand on your thighs first."

"Listen, drunk groping in college doesn't count." I laugh.

"Oh, it definitely does." She taps my leg. "Let's go. Show me the goods. Pretend it's already the honeymoon and tease me."

I roll my eyes but hike my dress up so she can put it on. The photographer loves it. I threaten to keep Valerie under my dress, but she pushes her way out. I help her up and she checks my nails, makes sure the back of my dress is where it's supposed to be, and takes my hands.

"You look beautiful, Sophia. Even if this dress is crazy." She laughs and squeezes my fingers in hers. Then her eyes narrow. "You took out the whole 'objections' part, right?"

I nod. "Of course we did. I don't need a surprise ex of one of my men jumping in and making a scene."

"Hell no. It's all about you." She kisses my cheek, laughs, and then has to get the makeup artist to help remove the lipstick.

After those finishing touches, we put the short veil in my hair, on top of all those curls. My mom holds my hands, looking me over as she tries not to cry.

Danny fluffs the back of my dress, now child-free, even though Gio is a delightful little thing. I take pictures with the girls and both of them look beautiful in their lavender dresses. I made sure they both approved before I got them.

"Are you ready to see your dad?" Mom asks.

I nod. We've eaten, had some champagne, and I feel ready to go, especially since I don't have to wear shoes until the reception. I turn in a circle and take a deep breath. Mom rushes out with a little giggle before calling him in a honey sweet voice.

Danny adjusts my sleeves and nods.

"Your guys are so ready for this," she whispers. "They're gushing already, and I'm pretty sure Gunner's already cried at least twice."

I nod, but my stomach is in a knot. "Did you feel all this pressure when you got married?"

"I felt *a* pressure." She pats her flat belly. "And someone who wouldn't stop kicking me."

"I just feel... Like I'm forgetting something important."

Danny looks around, then grabs four little sheets of paper. "Your vows."

I crush them against my chest and slip them into my dress, where they'll be covered. "I would have forgotten everything up there, I'm sure of it."

"It just spills out," she says. "I can't explain it. I wrote things and forgot to look at them. Massimo just winged it. He said the words were inside him the whole time and just needed an excuse to come out."

"What if something goes wrong? If it rains? If someone gets up or…"

"Hey." She motions Valerie over and they both take my hands. "This is the easiest part. You've done all the work, *enjoy* this."

"Yeah," Valerie says. "Stop focusing on the details and think about your men waiting for you. If you want, we can place bets on them crying, even though all of us know they're going to be blubbering … even if Danny and I have to kick them or something."

I laugh and sniff again. "I love you both. So much. All of this is happening so fast and I feel so emotional and chaotic and you're so helpful."

"That's why we're here," Valerie says in a sing-songy voice.

"Fuck yeah. And don't worry about anyone in the crowd. We will kick them out if you don't want them here. If I can handle pro soccer players and refs, I can handle some unruly guests." Danny promises me.

"Count me in on that too," Val says with a smile.

Their support is given, so loving, so sure that I feel shaken. How many people get this kind of chance in life? Marrying the person or people that they love with so much support and love surrounding the union? Especially before the wedding? How many people get to have more than they ever expected, things and people they never even thought to dream of or wish for?

"I'm going to cry already." I laugh, waving my hands in front of my face.

I'm so glad everything makeup-wise is waterproof or I know that I'd be ruined.

"Get out there and take pictures before the photographers get mad," Valerie orders.

I take a few pictures and I'm sure my dad is on the other side of the row of hedges. Then we look around to see each other. He smiles at me and I giggle. He comes all the way around, looks at me, and puts his hand to his face. His entire face goes red and splotchy, and his eyes water.

"Sophie." He holds his arms wide.

I sniff and then hug him tight, unable to *not*. "I love you, Daddy."

He squeezes me, then lets me go, only holding onto my hands. "My little girl."

I laugh, but a little sob leaves my throat, too. He shakes his head. "You're all grown up and getting married and so–so beautiful."

I grab two handfuls of the skirt and turn. "You like it?"

"I love it. I love *you*." He takes my hand and kisses the back of it. "And I love that you're going to make all four of them weep."

I laugh and look up at the sky, trying so hard not to cry this early. I haven't even gotten to the aisle. My mom and dad take photos with me. Then Valerie and Danny. After a bit, Gio is brought back. I don't even remember Danny slipping away.

He's featured in the photos with us and once we're done, I ask to hold him. Danny puts him in my arms and I bounce him a little. He reaches past me, grabbing a flower. I beam at him. "I know, it's beautiful, huh Gio?"

He tries to put it in his mouth, and I take it from him. He whimpers, but I kiss his forehead. "Be a good baby for me."

Softening his face, he gives me something close to a smile and I beam before handing him back to Danny. She cuddles him close, but then passes him to my mom so we three girls can take a few more pictures.

Then the photographer nods. I take more pictures with my parents, then a timer goes off.

I look at my dad and he takes my arm. My mom takes a deep breath and goes ahead to the seating area. I take a few deep breaths as flowers are put in my hands. Danny goes with Gio, her man. Then, when she's told to go, Valerie loops Massimo's arm.

"Your wife isn't going to kick me or something, is she?" Valerie asks.

"As long as your hands don't wander, you'll survive." He chuckles, love in his eyes as he watches his wife and son go down the aisle. "She's a fierce little thing, isn't she?"

I roll my eyes, but everything in me wants to follow right away and go to Roman. He has to be first, right? He's the one I'm with on paper. A shiver teases my spine and I take another deep breath.

"Sophie?"

I take a step back for a second, trying to calm down. Dad cups my face between his hands. "Second thoughts?"

"No!" I say, then lower my voice. "No, I'm just ... just overwhelmed."

He chuckles. "Take a few deep breaths, honey. You have all the time in the world."

My eyes flick up to him. "Liar."

He chuckles and strokes over my cheeks with his thumbs. "As much as I've given you and the guys hell, I know they love you. If you took an hour to get down the aisle each time, they'd still be there waiting for you, smiling, crying, all of it."

"But the guests. And I didn't check the reception hall and..." Another shaking breath leaves me.

Dad takes a few deep breaths and motions for me to do the same. He hugs me tight. "None of that matters. Not a damn thing matters other than how you feel. Do you want to do this? Are you *ready* to do this?"

"Yes," I say.

It's the only answer. Not because of all the deposits. Not because of all the work. Not because of the eyes watching. I know that the four men I love are waiting for me. Roman, Holden, Nick, and Gunner. They're going to take me in their arms, tell me everything that we'll have after today, and then ... and then I'll kiss them, promise them, my love, for as long as I live, and we can relax into our honeymoon and forever.

I close my eyes and picture them, holding me, hugging me, cooking together in the kitchen before game night. The way they proposed to me, us in Italy, us in Hawaii, and every moment we've shared in between.

With anyone else, six weeks to plan a wedding after less than a year together would be insane. I'd be trembling. I'd be second-guessing every decision that brought me here. I take a slow breath.

"I want to do it," I say, sure. "I want to, so bad."

"Four times," Dad says. "That's how many times we're walking down the aisle."

I nod and picture my fiancés. How strong and loving they are. The deeper sides to them I've seen. I take an unsteady breath and smile. "I want them. All of them. Just the aisle is ... intimidating."

My dad reaches into his jacket, then switches to the other side. He pulls out a piece of paper. "I don't know how this is supposed to help, but Nick gave it to me, just in case you started getting nervous."

My brow furrows and then I take the piece of paper, unfold it, and see a crayon drawing of a shark and a person swimming together. It's not great, it's silly, the shark is bright orange with spots of purple and it has a smile. The stick figure person has a claw-like hand on the shark and the sketchy blue background covers the whole page.

I sniff at it, then hold it to my chest. "It's perfect."

Dad shakes his head and puts his hand out for it. When I hesitate, he chuckles. "I'll give it back to you after the wedding, baby girl. You can take all the time you want in between; we'll need it since I'm going to be jogging around to pick you up again and walk again and again."

I laugh and wipe at my nose. My heart feels like it's going to burst into confetti, my legs don't feel very reliable, and my skin is hot all over. I can do this. More importantly, I *want* to do this. I want my men.

Dad and I get back into position, and I exhale. Everything in me is begging to sprint up the aisle, grab all four men and run away together, into the sunset like every romance book I've ever read.

But Dad loops my arm and nods to someone.

The music starts and after another slow breath, to calm everything in me and stop the tremors of excitement and nervousness, I take a step forward.

Here goes everything.

* * *

Need More!

Gunner Chapter 1

The music starts and all I can think about is everything that I've been through with every woman that's led to Sophie. I think about every opportunity that has led to this place, standing at the altar as her mother comes down the aisle, then Danny, then Valerie with Massimo's arm in hers.

I glance into the crowd, all seated for the *four* weddings that are taking place in sequence, and spot my family. My mother blows me a kiss as my dad dabs at the corner of his eyes. My sisters make kissy faces at me and stick out their tongues. I shouldn't expect anything less on my wedding day.

I stand a little taller and double-check the flower in my lapel. My eyes flick over to Matthew and Bella. Bella doesn't look half as pissy as I expected, considering how things went at her wedding, but I'm not complaining in the slightest. If anything, I'm relieved.

She won't be a problem. No one has crashed the wedding, unlike the rehearsal dinner, and the sun is bright and glorious in the sky with only a few white clouds to break up the blue. It's perfect. Getting ready was perfect. And we finally made it here.

I take a deep breath, sure the weight of the moment is going to flood my system when Sophie walks down the aisle, but there's a delay. One minute, another, a third, until the music starts. I glance at Massimo and he gives me a thumbs up, but I'm worried that Sophie will not be coming down the aisle. I'm worried it will just be her dad, coming to tell me the worst news.

But there she is.

"Holy fuck." I laugh.

I put my fist over my mouth and laugh as tears spring to my eyes. Sophie looks like a goddess. She's too good for me. That's never been clearer. She's beautiful, elegant, and beyond anything I could ever expect or hope for in a woman. She's a fucking angel, and she's giving herself to a mere mortal like me. It's humbling as hell.

"No way she's here for me." I take a shaky breath.

Massimo chuckles and pats my shoulder. Sophie's eyes water and she does the looking up trick I learned girls do to avoid ruining their makeup. When she gets to me, I'm still taking in the thick white skirt, the bodice that teases me with the low cut between her breasts, then her flushed face.

Her gorgeous eyes water as her auburn hair cascades in curls over one shoulder. After what feels like years, I reach for her hand. Miles stands between us, catching my notice for the first time. He doesn't say a word until Sophie elbows him, and then he hands her over with a grumble about trusting me with his daughter. Sophie kisses his cheek anyway when he steps back, allowing us to get closer.

The officiant speaks no words when it comes to her dad passing her off, just an exchange of hands and Miles saying, "I love you more than they ever can, honey."

I shake my head, but my smile spreads wide. Sophie takes my hand, walks with me to the altar, then brushes the tears from the corners of my eye. "Gunner, you're not allowed to cry."

"Too late, Sweets."

"If you cry, I'm going to cry and we're never going to get through our vows," she says and I see her mom laugh.

The officiant gets to work. He reads the poetry I selected for our wedding, says some other things that we knew were going to be said, and the whole time, I stroke Sophie's hands, squeeze her fingers between mine, mouth to her I love her, and try to distract her from the emotional speech. But her eyes are all misty and her face stays flushed, and it looks like there is glitter on her skin.

She's fucking enchanting. She, right here and now, is the whole definition of the word "love."

"Gunner, I believe you are reading your vows first," He says, looking at me.

I arch an eyebrow and Sophie nods. Fuck, she's going to destroy me if she goes first, so I'm damn determined to get through this, but I'm already nervous as hell to say things after choosing poetry for our ceremony. As if that's not enough to end my super-macho reputation, these vows are going to do it without question.

I take an unsteady breath. "Are you ready for it, Sophie?"

"Am I ever ready for you?" She squeezes my hand.

Clearing my throat, I pull out my notes. "Sweets, you have driven me insane since the moment I saw you. You knocked the wind out of me and I still haven't caught my breath around you. That you love my jokes, my flirting, my silly side, and make my heart burn with just a look has made it impossible for me to ignore you."

"Gun," she whispers.

"But then you inspired me to share more. To talk to you about my favorite books, to share the things I was taught no one would like. And the more I shared, the more you loved me. From reading romance together to planning surprise parties, to seeing you drunk and being together through the good and bad moments ... it's not enough. I need forever and I promise–I promise to love everything we have coming and to work through the difficult times without ever doubting you, your love, or your loyalty."

I see a tear work down her cheek and catch it with my finger. "You'll never have to cry alone, laugh alone, or spend a single day without knowing how much you mean to me. I can't wait to be your husband and I'm ready to say I DO right now."

She giggles and more tears slip. She takes a breath and dabs at her eyes.

"I might need an hour between weddings." She sniffs, her nose already red.

The audience laughs, and she takes a slow breath while sucking on her bottom lip. She peeks at me through her eyelashes and takes a step toward me. "Gunner, I can say I never saw you coming. You're like a shooting star, impossible to predict, and then … and then there. But you are …." Her face goes red again and her lips tremble. "You are *so* important to me."

I nod, trying to keep her going as her eyes shine with tears.

"I love you so much, and every time I think I know everything about you, you surprise me with something new. You never let me be sad for long because you can make me laugh no matter what I'm feeling. Whether it's dancing with me in the kitchen, whispering jokes in my ear when I'm nervous, holding me when I feel overwhelmed, or reminding me we can just run away and do something crazy, you make every day an adventure. You make me want so much more for myself and out of life."

God, my heart. It stutters in my chest, trying and failing to beat normally. I blink because she's going all watery and shake my head. I have to sniff, just to hold on to some bit of sanity. "Can I kiss you yet?"

"I promise, no matter how old we are, we're never going to grow up. I promise to never let you feel like you're an option when I can't live a day without you. I promise you that no matter what happens, I will always read with you, I will trust you, I will love you and I will *never* let you forget how much more you have to offer the world beyond your quick wit and cleverness."

I groan and try to pull her against me, but she giggles and shakes her head. "And I know you can be patient."

"Not with you," I argue. "Never with you, Sophie."

"Now, repeat after me …"

The classic lines are said, but Sophie doesn't promise obedience and I don't promise any kind of restraint. As soon as the rings are on, I try to kiss her again, making her giggle, but at least I have her against my chest now.

"You may now ..." Fuck, it's the longest pause in the entirety of the world. I can't handle it. I cup her face in my hand and run my nose over hers. "Kiss the bride."

"Fucking finally."

"Gun!" she squeaks at me, cursing, but I kiss the objection away.

I know it's supposed to be some romantic kiss that is family-friendly, but Sophie and I have never been and will never be capable of that kind of moderation. I kiss her like I'm dying and she's my last meal, pulling her up, so she has to stand on her toes and licking into her mouth.

There are some cheers, she draws back, her breath puffing against my cheek as she pants. Her nails dig into the back of my neck. "You're killing me, Gunner."

"A long slow waiting game isn't death, Sweets." I kiss her cheek. "I'm just giving you a taste of what you're going to have every morning before we part ways for work and every night before we go to sleep."

"I love you so much," she says. "So, so much. You're never an option. You're always a need."

I cup her face between my hands as she beams up at me, bright and so fucking perfect that I can't *not* kiss her again. I feel like the grinch when his heart grows three sizes. I didn't know it was possible to love her more than I have, but here I am, unable to believe that I've ever loved her any less.

"I'm all yours, Sophie."

"Better not tell me that," she teases. "Or I'm going to make some naughty demands."

I laugh and hold our hands up. My parents whistle and my sisters whoop. Sophie's mom stands and hugs us both, but then her dad follows us back down the aisle. The officiant reminds everyone that there is an open bar, but not to leave the area since we'll be starting all over again in less than thirty minutes.

"God, thirty minutes isn't enough for me to get under this dress and ravage you," I groan.

"Still here," Miles grumbles, but only at half venom.

He looks between us, then hugs me, patting my shoulder. "That was great, Gunner. Really good. Keep those promises, so I don't have to kill you."

"I think there would be a lineup for my head if I ever hurt Sophie." I wink at her over her dad's shoulder.

He nods and I see him wipe at his eyes. "God damn, I'm not ready for round Two, Sophie. I'm not."

"It's okay, Daddy." She hugs him.

"I'm going to be walking your next man in," I say when Sophie tries to take my hand.

"But!" It's a quick complaint.

I fix the little smears to her makeup and press my forehead to hers. "But nothing. You'll have us all soon enough. And you're more than worth the wait."

She melts and kisses me again. "Who is it?"

"It's a secret," I tease. "Now be good and dry those eyes."

"Fat chance." She fans at her face.

I nod to Miles and head around to join Massimo at the altar. He hands me some whiskey and I nod in thanks. It's going to be an emotional fucking day. Massimo finishes his drink and glances at people sitting back down.

"Do you think Nick is ready?"

"Not a fucking chance. I'm still recovering." I wave at my face. "I'm glad I don't have to do it four times."

"Better make it worth it for Sophie tonight." Massimo winks then slaps my ass to get me back in place for round two.

Sophia Chapter 2

Valerie hands me some champagne and I take a slow drink. It's in celebration, not in panic. But I didn't plan for Gunner to make me cry. Now I feel like a soggy mess.

"Daddy," I whimper.

"Your makeup is fine, honey." He promises, adjusting a lock of hair. "One down, three to go."

"I think my heart might explode into confetti before then. How can I handle so much affection?" I pant.

"Get used to it. I have a feeling they're going to drown you in it for the rest of your life," he says.

His soft smile, the watery eyes, and his red cheeks make me feel a million times better.

Danny and her baby head down the aisle, then Valerie and Mass, which leaves me and Dad. The music changes and here we go again. It's Nick. Nick, who's waiting for me and looking as gorgeous as expected, his slightly graying hair blowing in the light breeze as his eyes widen, then go all squinted as he beams. I keep my smile, but I know I'm crying by the time I reach the altar.

Gunner stands with Massimo beside him and I know by the time I get to my number four, I'm going to be a mess. Gunner wipes at his eyes again, as if he didn't *just* marry me and Dad hands me over a little easier to Nick, patting his shoulder before sitting down with my mom.

Nick helps me up the last two steps. He looks me over, head to toe and back at least three times, noticing all the different little details. "Sophia…"

And he's just as fabulous, so has no room to talk. The perfectly fitted tux, the way he has a warm color to highlight his skin, the glint in his eyes, the almost messy, sexy look he has going on. It makes my knees weak.

"I'm not going to remind everyone why we're here again," The officiant jokes.

Nick laughs. "It is a wedding, right?"

I giggle. I let the guys pick passages of poetry or whatever they want to be included before the vows since I selected the songs and I already know Nick's is different. Gunner was poetry, Nick is … all about love, the fundamentals, the quotes.

"Love is what we make of it, but there is one truth that remains—it is the easiest and hardest thing you will ever do. There are days when you will have to love your partner one hundred percent because they just don't have it in them to love even themselves. There are days you'll be fifty-fifty. The most important thing to remember is to choose your person every day, no matter their mood. Choose them in the morning, choose them in the good times and bad. Choose them when you would rather run away. Keep choosing them and your marriage will never fail—and your love will endure."

I'm already crying. Nick cups my face in his hand, wiping my tear and earning a quivering kiss to his palm. The officiant encourages us to say our vows, but this time I'm going first.

"Nick!" I hiss.

He motions again. "Hit me with it, sweetheart. I'm ready."

I'm not. Not with that sweet smile that lights up his face, the love that radiates out from him, the warmth, everything that's so soft and welcoming, and ... Fuck, I'm so screwed. How am I supposed to string a sentence together?

"I.." I purse my lips, wipe my eyes, and start again. "I don't know where to start with you, Nick. You've made your way into my heart day by day. You're so damn consistent, so warm and understanding. You keep the peace between us all and you do it in a way that just makes you essential to my happiness."

He nods.

"And yet, you keep finding more ways to prove what an amazing match we are. Sharing your fun facts, planning ways for us to spend time together that take us out of the house, letting me support you as much as you support me, and never *ever* making me feel stupid. Even when we fight, you make me think and I love that I will always be able to learn with you, grow with you, and I only hope that I offer you as much as you offer me."

"Soph-"

I put my hand over his mouth. "You get your turn. Hush." He smiles and kisses my fingers. I take a steadying breath, as if I'm not crying. "I promise never to raise my voice in anger again or lash out at you. I promise to work to be patient and to follow through on every one of my ideas for hobbies we can do. I'll paint with you, I'll support every dream you have, and I will *never* let you feel unwanted. There's no way my life could ever be complete without you, your trust, and your love."

I remove my hand and he takes it in his own and kisses my knuckles. He opens his mouth and I shake my head. "One second. I'm going to lose all my makeup."

He laughs with the crowd and helps me control my eyes by whispering a shark fact in my ear, which makes me laugh and tear up all over again. "Thank you for the note."

"I love you, Sophia. I love your dedication and the fact that you're independent and determined. You never slow down or let up when it comes to what you want, and I'm damn lucky you want me. Any night that I haven't been able to be with you, any morning when I've *just* missed you before work kills me. I can't even think of a life without you."

Oh god. My legs are shaking. He's holding on so tight, his lips quivering as if the idea is so devastating he doesn't even want to say it. "This is harder than it looks, by the way."

Gunner pats his shoulder and he continues. "You make me want to be a better man every day. You remind me that there is so much more to life than working, eating, and living for the weekend. But even weeknights feel magical with you. You make everything new and exciting, and I can't believe I'm lucky enough to get to have you for the rest of my life. I promise I will be an active part of your life and I promise I will never let work overshadow our life together. I will never miss dinner again."

We finish with the standard ring exchange and I'm in Nick's arms before the officiant can announce it. After I come up from one toe-curling kiss, he gets it out before Nick kisses me back. One arm locked around my waist and his hand cupping the back of my head. He behaves a hell of a lot more than Gunner did, but it's still too much to handle.

I feel like I'm going to choke on a sob when he pulls away. Nick strokes down the sides of my neck and then to my hands. He holds me, sliding his arm around my waist, then turning and holding his hand up as I show off my flowers. Everyone cheers and I see Nick's parents. His mother is crying, wearing a flower crown, while his dad looks confused.

Nick kisses the top of my head. "Are you happy, Sophie?"

I nod. "I'll let you know when I can catch my breath," I say.

As we walk back down the aisle, Gunner follows. Nick shoves him toward the bar and asks him to choose a drink. Gunner flashes finger guns before walking away. Nick rolls his eyes and kisses me again, working his tongue into my mouth until I feel like I'm going to just float away on pleasure and happiness.

"Do you have any idea how much I love you?" he asks.

"Enough to have my dad pass the best note I've ever received when I needed it the most?"

I stroke over his tux jacket. "I have this idea that we paint all the adventures we have. All the trips we go on together."

He picks me up, making me squeal, then wraps his arms under my bottom. I'm kind of shocked he found it, and my dress is all bunched around his chest, so he looks like he's ready for a photo op with no background.

I fix his hair, but his smile is so winning, he's so happy that I already have my answer before he says anything. "I love it. I love you."

"I love you so much."

He lets me down, so I slide down his body and the amount of fabric between us doesn't matter. Lust pools low in my stomach, and by the time he sets me on my bare feet, I'm rubbing against him while panting.

"Sophie," he whispers, the slightest tilt of a warning to his voice. "Not yet."

"I'm so impatient. You can make me come in fifteen minutes." I press a kiss to his throat. "You have before."

He groans and kisses across my forehead, my temple, my nose, and then my lips. Hungry, but then he draws back. "We agreed. Not until after the *reception*."

"Boring," I grumble.

"You know how much I like the rules."

"You broke them before," I say.

He adjusts my veil and then I see my dad standing right there with his eyebrow raised, arms crossed over his chest. I swallow hard. "Hi, Daddy."

"And *what* rules were broken?"

"Put your work face away." I huff. "We kissed within a week of the wedding which was against the rules. And I don't regret it." I poke Nick's chest.

He kisses me again, winks, and walks away. Dad shakes his head at me. "You're killing me, honey."

"I'm sorry, Daddy."

He cranes his neck and rolls his eyes. "And your mother is coming onto your husbands."

"Hey!" I pick up my skirt in my hands, but Dad stops me. He whistles once and I see Danny perk up. She gives my dad a thumbs up and I laugh. "You're sicking Danny on her?"

"It's effective." He shrugs in a way that says he's not the least bit sorry. "Your mother needs to learn some self-control."

"And you will not give me even a hint when it comes to who's next?" I put a hand on my hip.

"You decided to marry four of them and didn't specify an order. Would that make it any easier?"

I peek around to the bar where Massimo, Gunner, and Nick are toasting each other. I'm so happy to see them glowing the way they are. Gunner and Nick hug and show each other their bands–each of my men have different ones–and then I put my band in Dad's hand.

He nods to me, kisses my cheek, and has the makeup artist check my face again. Waterproof makeup my ass. It's not love-proof which means I'm fucked. Totally fucked. It might have lasted through one wedding, but I'm two in and only halfway there.

"Round three."

"Want to make a bet on who it is?"

I feel something like a calm spread over me and meet Dad's eyes as my procession walks down the aisle. "It's Holden."

"You sound sure."

Honestly, I don't know why I am, but somehow I know. And it pulls a huge smile and sure steps from me. Nervous or not, I know Holden is the calm force I need.

Need More!

ALSO BY BARBI COX

Also by Barbi Cox In order of publication

The Billionaire's Obsession - **An Age Gap Curvy girl Best Friend Ménage ROMCOM**

Lovestruck- **An Age Gap Forbidden Brother Ménage**

Ménage in the City (Box set including The Billionaire's Obsession and Lovestruck)

Romance Goals Series

Fake Fiancée Goals Steamy enemies to lovers curvy girl

Dirty Daddy Goals Age gap, I'll have your dad story.

Enemies with Benefits Goals Enemies to lovers

Friends with Benefits Goals Friends to lovers

Bay Boy Players (Box set includes 4 books above)

Romance Goals Series- must be read in order

Their Temptation Series- Must be read in order

Age Gap, Ex Military, Reverse Harem

Prequel - Their Sugar Baby

Daddy's 4 Dirty Friends

Shared by Daddy's 4 Dirty Friends

Loved by Daddy's 4 Dirty Friends

Claimed by Daddy's 4 Dirty Friends

Taken by Daddy's 4 Dirty Friends

Touched by Daddy's 4 Dirty Friends

Spoiled by Daddy's 4 Dirty Friends

Unwrapped by Daddy's 4 Dirty Friends

Devoured by Daddy's 4 Dirty Friends

Ravished by Daddy's 4 Dirty Friends

Bound by Daddy's 4 Dirty Friends

Craved by Daddy's 4 Dirty Friends

Three For Me Series - Age Gap Reverse Harem Dark Mafia Romance.

Must be read in order

Charmed by 3

Seduced by 3

Claimed by 3

Owned by 3

Adored by 3

Shared by 3

Treasured by 3

Their Forbidden Fruit Series - Age Gap Dad's Best Friend Dark Mafia Romance.

Must be read in order

Daddy's Devil

Daddy's Angel

Age Gap Dad's Best Friend Single Dad Mafia Romance

Three Men One Love

Small Town Bad Boys Cops and Cowboys - Age Gap Ex-Military Stepbrother Romance

Wild

Wild Hearts

Stand Alone

[The Billionaire's Obsession](#)

[Lovestruck](#)

[Three Men One Love](#)

[Her Dad's Billionaire Ex Bestie](#)

Barbi Cox and Olivia King - Mafia Romance

The Bratva Billionaires' Forbidden Darlings

[Stolen Hearts](#)

[Stolen Kisses](#)

[Stolen Moments](#)

[Stolen Desires](#)

Mafia Enemies to Lovers

Mafia Lover

[Join my readers group](#)

[Secret Facebook Group](#)

www.ingramcontent.com/pod-product-compliance
Lightning Source LLC
Chambersburg PA
CBHW020945040825
30574CB00007B/19